DEAD AND ALIVE

DEAD
AND
ALIVE

Photis George

Matador
Unit E2 Airfield Business Park,
Harrison Road, Market Harborough,
Leicestershire. LE16 7UL
Tel: 0116 279 2299
Email: books@troubador.co.uk
Web: www.troubador.co.uk/matador
Twitter: @matadorbooks

ISBN 978 1803131 061

British Library Cataloguing in Publication Data.
A catalogue record for this book is available from the British Library.

Printed and bound in Great Britain by 4edge Limited
Typeset in 11pt Minion Pro by Troubador Publishing Ltd, Leicester, UK

Matador is an imprint of Troubador Publishing Ltd

ONE

Benedict opened his eyes. His head was pounding so loudly he could not hear himself think. He was sitting on a very cold stone floor, up against a damp wall. He tried to stand but his legs buckled beneath him, and he slumped back down again and fell onto this cold dampness that was enveloping his entire body.

He closed and opened his eyes a few times, but all was total darkness. He was starting to feel frightened. Very, very, frightened.

Benedict was a tall, athletic looking boy of seventeen years, with dark brown hair and piercing blue eyes. Ben, as he liked to be called, was quite used to looking after himself, as his father who was a scientist, would disappear for days at a time, locking himself in his laboratory in the basement of their South London home.

OK, Ben, keep calm and think back. What is the last thing you can remember? All that kept coming into his head were two bright flashes and a thunderous noise.

Suddenly he could hear distant voices getting louder, and footsteps on the wet stone.

His heart started to thump loudly as the voices grew louder and the footsteps closer. The footsteps stopped and he could now make out what they were saying and see some light under the door.

"Ratzilla said we must dispose of the body before it starts to smell"

"How will Ratzilla persuade the boy's father to finish the nerve gas if the boy is dead?"

"The professor won't know," said the first voice.

Benedict heard what sounded like a key going into a metal lock and start to turn. He was so scared that his heart was now beating so fast he thought it would explode. As the door slowly creaked open, he fell back through the solid wall and was now lying in a smelly tunnel.

What is happening to me? Ben thought. *I'm not blind, that's great, but what just happened, and where are my clothes?*

Ben stood up, his legs still a bit shaky. He looked to his left. Nothing but darkness. Then to his right, where he saw a faint light in the distance. Ben headed towards the light.

Ben walked naked for a few minutes, ankle deep in cold dirty waters, his eyes getting used to the darkness. Ben stopped. He thought he could hear voices echoing down the tunnel walls.

"How can a dead boy escape from a locked cell?" one voice said. "And why would he leave all his clothes behind. Unless he wasn't dead at all."

"But Ratzilla said he was dead" the other voice said.

"Oh, and Ratzilla is the Brains of Britain, is he? So how did he escape from a locked cell? We'll ask Ratzilla, as you think he knows everything, dimwit."

"Maybe he dug a tunnel," came the reply.

"The only thing with a tunnel is your brain, Andrew. Just keep going down the sewer or Ratzilla will kill us both."

"OK Andreas," said Andrew.

"I'll call Andros and Andy and let them know, they can get down here and help us find this kid," Andreas said.

Ben turned and carried on towards the light, but after a few minutes, he could hear more voices coming towards him from the other direction.

As the voices started to get louder and closer, both in front and behind, he started to get more scared, even telling his heart to stop beating so loudly, because he thought they would be able to hear it. He started to run.

He could see a light up ahead, which was pouring through the drain grate above. The men chasing him were running too and shouting to each other not to let him escape.

Ben saw a ladder above his head and jumped for the bottom rung but did not get high enough and missed. The men were now closing in on him. Ben steadied himself for another try, his heart beating so fast he was having trouble breathing. He was scared, so scared, even more scared than when he had ruined one of his father's experiments by being in the lab without permission.

He jumped again with all his might, but instead of catching the ladder, he flew up the chute and through the metal grate onto the road above. Ben was now floating in mid-air, about three feet above the damp ground, below the bright light of the lamp post that had guided him to that spot. The road was a typical high street with shops on either side, quiet, with no traffic going past.

"What is happening to me?" he shouted. A couple standing at the bus stop opposite did not flinch as if they could neither see nor hear him. As their bus arrived, they got on board, and it drove away.

Meanwhile, back down below ground, Andrew shakily climbed onto Andros shoulder with help from Andreas and Andy. Andrew pushed as hard as he could, but he was unable to open the grate above. After a few more unsuccessful attempts, Andrew dropped to the wet tunnel floor. The four all stared at each other in the gloomy light, nobody wanting to speak first as they all knew they were in big trouble. Eventually Andros sheepishly said:

"Ratzilla is going to kill us all."

"It wasn't my fault" Andy added. "It was you two who were sent to fetch the boy from his cell," pointing to Andrew and Andreas.

"How can it be our fault" Andrew replied. "He escaped from a locked cell then flew up into the air and through a closed grate that won't budge"

"Yeah" said Andreas.

"Well, it wasn't our fault," Andy and Andros said in unison.

"It's none of our faults," shouted Andrew. By now all four were trying to shout louder than each other.

"Ratzilla is going to kill us for sure now," said a trembling voice. The four turned and made their way back to Ratzilla.

Ben breathed a sigh of relief as his naked body gently came down to earth outside an estate agents shop. Ben could hear raised voices coming from the drain grate. Noticing his naked body reflecting from the shop window, Ben quickly ran to the charity shop ten metres away where carrier bags had been dumped outside. Ben started to rummage through the bags until he found some clothes, but it was all women's stuff. After cursing his luck, he decided on a white blouse, some very large knickers, and a dark blue thick and warm overcoat. He drew the line at wearing a dress he might be desperate, but he still had his pride.

Ben started to walk as he had no way of paying for a bus let alone a taxi, even if he knew where he was going.

—

The four men below ground trundled their way through the dark wet sewer.

"How can it be possible?" Andreas asked.

"How can what be possible?" Andrew replied.

"The boy got out of a locked cell, and why did he leave all his clothes. It don't make sense," Andreas continued.

"Yeah, and then get through that grate without opening it," said Andros. "He is slim but not that slim".

"I don't know who scares me more, Ratzilla or the boy," Andy interrupted.

"Do you think he will get the police now he has escaped?" asked Andreas.

"Definitely" Andrew replied. "He will come back with the police to save his father."

"Why don't we just get away and leave Ratzilla to face the music?" Andros stated.

"Because Ratzilla knows where we live, and he will come after us for sure" Andrew replied.

"And I don't want to be shot with that gun," Andy stated.

The four cousins returned to Ratzilla's lair which was at least above ground and dry. The abandoned warehouse was just a collection of corrugated iron rooms with fluorescent lights flickering every now and again. Andrew summoned up the courage to give Ratzilla, who was standing in the middle of the room dressed all in black, holding the gun in both hands and had a face like thunder, the news that the boy was alive and had escaped. Ratzilla raised the weapon up and pointed it at them.

"How could he be alive! He was dead, I checked his pulse myself" Ratzilla raged.

"Please boss, don't use it on us, we'll find him", said Andreas. "He's only a kid, where can he hide?"

Ratzilla turned a small dial on the side of the weapon, pointed it at Andrew, and fired. Andrew froze.

"Your cousin is not dead yet" said Ratzilla, "but he will be if you don't bring that boy back to me. I don't care if the boy is dead or alive, just bring him back here. Go back to his house and wait for him. He's only a boy, he can't go to the police, they would more likely lock him up in an institution than believe him, so where else can he go?"

Andreas nodded turned and walked out of the room, quickly followed by Andros and Andy.

"Those fools" Ratzilla mumbled to himself as the three cousins left the warehouse. "They have the combined I.Q of a pigeon, but they are cheap" he sighed.

TWO

It was a crisp, dry, August morning. After walking for a couple of hours through the quiet streets of London, Ben came to the embankment of the River Thames just as it was getting light. At least he knew where he was now, but he couldn't go home. They, whoever they were, would surely be waiting for him. He found a bench and tried to sleep but he couldn't; everything that had happened that night was going round and round his head making no sense at all.

Ben walked over Albert Bridge, it was his favourite bridge where his mother used to bring him and tell him stories about the stars and the planets. He had not been back for twelve years. It had lost its magic after his mother had died.

He stopped in the middle of the bridge and looked up to the skies as if he would be able to see his mother and she would tell him what to do next.

The bridge started to get busier with people going to work, all staring at this young boy, wondering what sort of prank he had been on the wrong end of, to be here dressed as he was. There were a lot more cars going past now.

Ben decided to visit his best friend Angus. Ben had always considered Angus to be the cleverest person after his father.

Benedict arrived at Angus' large Victorian South London house at 8.00am hoping for help, some clothes and breakfast; he was starving. The one thing he hadn't lost was his appetite.

After ringing the doorbell five times and waiting ten minutes, Angus eventually came to the door. Ben knew he would take a long time to answer as Angus' sprawling bedroom was on the top floor.

"What are you doing up and about before midday during the summer holidays?" Angus enquired of his friend whilst rubbing his eyes. Then noticing what Ben was wearing, he burst out laughing hysterically then stopped abruptly. "Why was I not invited to the fancy dress party?" he said quite angrily. "You always get invited to the best parties, Ben, why didn't you call me?".

"Can I come in, please, Angus? I need your help," Ben mumbled to his friend. "Are your parents in?"

"No, they are at work I think," Angus replied.

Angus was slim but not as tall as Ben and had wavy blonde hair that had a mind of its own. He was also an only child, which is another thing the two friends had in common.

Angus Sinclair and Ben had been friends since they were four years old when they started school together and had always been on the same wavelength.

Angus made his friend a cup of tea and gave him a bowl of cereal. They may be good friends, but Angus doesn't cook for anyone. The boys then made their way up three flights of stairs to Angus' bedroom. It wasn't a typical room for a seventeen-year-old. Two very large bookshelves full of reference books of all types. No posters on the wall of pop groups or girls, but pictures of the solar system and planets.

Benedict started to tell his friend everything that had happened to him since he woke up in the dark damp cell.

At first, Angus thought his friend had been smoking some sort of wacky backy, but he knew Ben too well. He would not touch the stuff because his father had shown him what his insides would turn to if he smoked or touched it. Angus had been making notes of everything Benedict had said and had underlined two sentences.

After pausing for a couple of minutes Angus stood up, and with pen in his mouth pretending it was a pipe, he started to pace up and down the room, deliberately trying to look like Sherlock Holmes.

"Well," said Angus. "There are two parts of this story that make no sense at all." He was now starting to sound like Sherlock Holmes.

"Firstly", Angus said as he stopped in front of Ben removing the pen from his mouth, "Are you sure there was no trap door in the cell, and you accidently opened it and fell through it? We will deal with the clothes or lack of later".

"No definitely not," said Ben. "I would have seen the opening and the men who came to get me from the cell would have seen it too and followed me into the sewer".

"So how did they know you were in the sewer?" said Angus, staring at his friend.

"They must have heard me splashing through the water", Ben said. "I don't know do I, it's all so very confusing, I didn't wait to ask them, did I?" Ben added.

"Secondly, and most puzzling of all", deliberated Angus. "Is how you escaped out of the sewer. You said you flew straight up and out through the closed grill and landed 5 metres up on the road. Floating above the ground and two people standing at a bus stop opposite just ignored you as if you were not there!"

"Yes Angus," said Ben. "That's exactly what happened".

"Ben, I do believe you," said Angus. "And I think I know what has happened to you". He paused for a moment, took a deep breath. "You had a bad dream my friend, and you cross dress in your sleep".

With that Angus started to laugh loudly.

Ben stood up. He was not impressed with his friend and started to get very angry. "I was not dreaming!" he shouted. As he said this, his coat came undone, and his large undergarment became visible to his friend.

With this Angus started to laugh uncontrollably.

By now Ben was seething with rage, his heart pounding away furiously.

Angus suddenly stopped laughing and the colour drained out of him instantly. He could not believe his eyes. Ben had just vanished right in front of him. All that was left of Ben was a large white blouse, a blue coat, and some knickers: very large knickers. Angus just slumped down in his desk seat with a look of total disbelief and could not utter a word.

Ben saw his friend react this way and wondered why. Then he realised he was floating above the ground naked again.

THREE

James Ratsby came from South London. He was born in 1958, an only son of a gentlemen's barber and a seamstress. James was a scrawny boy as a child, jet black hair and piercing blue eyes. His parents both worked very hard to keep a roof over their heads and put food on the table. They lived in a tiny two-up-two-down with a tiny back yard, with no outside space to play or bring back friends. Although he never went without, he never had any luxuries and was always dreaming of becoming rich and famous. James was a bright boy but never really excelled at anything. He was OK at most things at school but not good enough to get into any of the sports teams or top streams. The one thing he was good at was daydreaming, so much so, he never really had any close friends at school, but this did not bother him at all. James would always be found in a corner of the school playground, dreaming about one thing or another. That's when he came up with the name Ratzilla; it was similar to his name but more menacing. A real villain's name. People would take him seriously if he used that name.

James' first brush with the authorities came when he was 8 years old. It was during the summer holidays of 1966. England had just won the world cup and the whole country was still celebrating, except for his mother and father who had no television and had no interest in football. James was ordered to go out and play by his mother so she could carry on with her sewing (she worked from home) and she needed the space to hang up the finished dresses. After three weeks of the holidays, James was bored and hungry. He was not allowed crisps or sweets between meals, only fruit and he didn't like fruit, because fruit is good for you, his mother would always say. James crept back into the house and into his mother's bedroom where he found her handbag. He quietly opened it and pulled out her purse. Inside the purse he only found coins a few pennies and one shiny silver half crown. James knew he could buy a lot of sweets and crisps with that shiny coin, but his mother would know it was missing and his father would punish him severely when he got home if he stole it. James sat crossed legged on the floor and dreamt of what he could buy with this wonderful shiny coin.

Whilst in his own little world James had an idea; he noticed that the half crown was about the same size as the penny but a little thicker. Sneaking quietly into the kitchen James went over to the window where his mother would keep the clean empty milk bottles ready to be put out that evening for the milkman to replace with full bottles of milk the next morning. James also knew his mother had a habit of cleaning the silver bottle tops and saving them; why she saved them he did not know but he did know that there were always plenty in a dish by the window and the clean bottles. James took two and crept back to the bedroom where he also took the half-crown and one penny from his mother's purse. He then carefully replaced the purse in his mother's handbag. James crept out to the front of his house and hid behind the dustbins in the front garden. He then proceeded to smooth out the silver milk bottle tops using the edge of the penny. Once both silver tops were smooth, he placed one over the half-crown and rubbed the queens head impression onto the silver foil. He then repeated the process for the other side of the half-crown. Once he was happy both sides looked realistic, he carefully wrapped the penny with the silver foil, smoothing down the edges and pressing tight to make sure you could not see any rough ends of foil.

James looked at the finished coin and smiled; Perfect, he thought. He then crept back into his mother's bedroom and replaced the half-crown in his mother's purse.

"Now off to spend my fortune," he said to himself. A few hundred yards from where James lived was the local sweet shop. James rarely went inside but would often stand outside and enviously look inside at the lucky children who had money to buy sweets. He now was one of those lucky children and boldly went inside, as if he owned the shop. James proceeded to pick up sweets and crisps by the handful, placing them onto the counter and asking the shopkeeper to let him know when he had reached half a crown's worth. The shopkeeper was happy to oblige; He had just doubled his days takings and was not going to ask the young boy any questions. James handed the man his forged half-crown without showing any nerves. The shopkeeper took the coin, and after a quick glance put it in his till and shut the draw. Then he put all the sweets into a large carrier bag and handed it over to James, who calmly said thank you and walked out the door. I'm going to be rich, he thought to himself as he walked down the road. James went to the local park where most of the children he knew from school were playing and started to sell the sweets at half price. What he couldn't sell, he ate.

That night James couldn't sleep as he dreamt of all the money he was going to make. He jumped out of bed the next morning, as soon as he heard his father go to work and his mother's sewing machine start buzzing. James snuck into his mother's room, took out the purse and removed the half-crown again, then went into the kitchen and took another two silver milk bottle tops, went outside, and proceeded to make another forged half-crown. After replacing the half-crown, he proceeded to make his way out of the house and spend his new coin. This is where it all started to go wrong for James. He returned to the same sweet shop but this time, as soon as he stepped inside the door, the shopkeeper from behind the counter grabbed hold of him by the arm and said:

"I thought you would be back young man; the coin you gave me yesterday fell apart in the till, you tricked me and now you are going to pay." The shopkeeper then called the police, who marched James home and told his mother everything that had happened. She was mortified; they had never been in trouble with the police before. James' mother marched him back to the shop and paid the shopkeeper for all the sweets he'd had the previous day, using her one and only half-crown.

"Your father will deal with you when he gets home from work."

James knew his only mistake was going back to the same shop; crime does pay if you are smart, he thought. From that day onwards, school was no longer important; James only concentrated on making easy money.

James Ratsby left school having failed all his exams; he was a major disappointment to both his parents who would often argue and blame each other for the way James had turned out. He worked with his father for one day, but deliberately made mistakes so he would not have to go back. He even made a mess of sweeping the barber's shop, leaving most of the cut hair on the floor. Forced to go out to work by his parents, he stumbled from one job to the next. This went on for a number of years, then one day he came across a deserted warehouse near Paddington, making it his home and base for his wheeler-dealing.

James never found out who owned the warehouse. *Must be the local council*, he thought, *and they didn't know it was theirs, never paid rent or anything, not even electricity.* It was off everyone's radar.

James was just as unsuccessful with the ladies and had become even more of a recluse; he hadn't seen his parents in years but was happy to do his own thing, and still dreaming of hitting the big time even now in his fifties. That was James, still dreaming, but still no nearer to making his fortune. Now calling himself Ratzilla, but still dreaming.

FOUR

Ratzilla was neither large in stature nor in personality, just a greying nobody who was going nowhere fast. All this had changed four weeks earlier when he received a package at his derelict base.

"Who would send me a package?"

He put his ear to the box just in case it was ticking. Ratzilla smiled with relief when it wasn't . There was no name or return address on the package. *Strange,* he thought. *How did it get here? Must have been hand delivered.* He carefully opened the box to find a shiny metal object that looked like a gun, but not like anything he had seen before. There was also a computer disc. *Instructions,* he hoped. *Some poor mug has ordered this and it's been sent here by mistake. It looks expensive,* he thought,

"I might make a few quid," he said out loud.

Ratzilla looked around him; he did not want anyone seeing him in the local library. *What would people think?* he thought, as he tipped his hat down and adjusted his dark glasses. But this was no good, he couldn't see a thing. After fiddling with the library computer, he managed to get the disc that had been sent to him with the gun to work. The computer disc contained instructions on the gun but also what he needed to do to repay his generous benefactors for giving him the gun. It was meant for him, after all. He briefly wondered why he had been chosen, but as an answer was not immediately forthcoming, he thought there was no point in dwelling on the issue.

After printing the instructions off he returned to his base to play with his new toy.

First, place the weapon in the desired hand. Turn red dial with another hand. Another hand? I've only got one hand left, must be a typo, he thought. *Turn red dial towards you and press button gently. Once this is completed nobody else can use this weapon. Turn red dial top to stun, turn dial towards what you are shooting to extinguish life, turn dial to down position to unstun person*. Ratzilla read the remaining instructions, but his mind was only on trying out his new gun. *If this thing is real, the world is mine; well North West London anyway.*

I need money, Ratzilla thought, *lots of money, and some henchmen; all villains need some henchmen. Everyone in London will be scared of me, he thought.* At that moment, the cat he had got, to catch all the rats that came up from the basement and sewers, woke from its slumber and stretched its legs before going to find some food. Ratzilla turned the dial to stun, pointed it at the cat and pressed the button. A bright white flash lit up the room and the cat just stopped in its tracks. Ratzilla walked over to the cat and poked it; the cat was still breathing but was not moving. Ratzilla turned the dial to face down and aimed at the cat. Again, there was a bright white flash, and the cat ran off. At this point

Ratzilla realised just how much power he now had and that he must do what the people who sent this to him want. The thought of double crossing them entered his mind but only for a split second because deep down Ratzilla was a coward; he still slept with the light on.

Ratzilla walked to the local high street disguised with a hat and dark glasses. Next to the charity shop was the local pawnbrokers. *They have lots of money*, he thought, *let's see this thing really work.* On entering the shop, which had a very large counter with a large glass bandit screen going all the way to the ceiling, he looked to see how many people were working.

"Afternoon", came a voice from behind the counter. Without hesitating he took out the gun, which he had pre-set to stun, as he didn't want to kill anyone.

"We don't give money out on kids toys", came the voice from behind the counter, "only gold and electrical goods".

Ratzilla raised the gun and pressed the button. The shop was lit up with white light, and this poor man was frozen stiff behind the counter. It then dawned on Ratzilla that the money was the other side of a locked counter, and he had no way of getting to it. This was not working as he had planned. That was the problem; he had no plan. Ratzilla turned the dial to unstun, pointed it at the sales assistant, and pressed the button. The man carried on with his sales speech about what was acceptable to pawn and what was not. Ratzilla just turned and walked out a bit embarrassed, but happy his gun worked on humans as well as cats.

FIVE

Eventually Ratzilla had worked out that robbing places without locked counters and security screens was a lot more profitable, and had accumulated a large amount of cash in a short space of time. Ratzilla was looking around his local computer shop to buy a computer, rather than steal, because he needed it to be set up for him. Whereas, if he stole it, he would not be able to get it working. Ratzilla was now planning everything. Whilst in the shop these three yobs came in, and they did not look like shoppers. One of the men handed the girl on the cash desk an envelope with the words "This is a robbery give us all the money" written on one side. The girl turned over the envelope, laughed, and pressed the alarm. Before the men could run Ratzilla stunned the cashier and security guard, opened the till draw for the men, and took the note the robbers had given the cashier.

They turned to Ratzilla in utter amazement.

"Wow man, how did you do that?" said the man who handed the note to the cashier.

"Never you mind, just follow me if you don't want to be arrested", said Ratzilla. They all ran out and jumped into a waiting car with its engine running outside the shop. Ratzilla turned and unstunned his two victims in the computer store, just as the car drove off.

Back at the warehouse, Ratzilla asked them who had written the robbery note on the envelope they gave the cashier.

"I did", said a voice.

"Who is Andreas Andrew?", asked Ratzilla.

"I am," replied the same voice. "How do you know my name?" he asked.

"It's written on the other side of the envelope with your address, that's why the cashier pressed the alarm you idiot."

"Don't call my cousin an idiot, he's just a bit slow that's all." one of the other men said. "We are all cousins; our parents came to England from Cyprus."

Andreas introduced his cousins to Ratzilla.

Totally confused, he demanded they call him Ratzilla.

"I have some things I need to do, and I need some help. If you want to make lots of money and never work again, all you have to do is what I tell you without question. If not, I will turn this gun on you all, right now."

"No mister, we'll do as you say, please don't kill us!" the four said in unison.

"Right then," said Ratzilla. "Just do as I say at all times, and I will make you all very rich."

The four cousins were all born in London of Greek Cypriot parents, who had left their small village to seek their fortunes in England. Unfortunately, one of the many things the four cousins have in common is they are all lacking any intellectual genes. When the brains were being handed out, these four were at the back of the queue . The four had struggled through school and work, so they spent their days driving around causing trouble whilst trying to make a fast buck here and there. On one particular day, the four were driving through central London in a battered up old car when they noticed a police car following them.

"Stop looking round at the police," Andreas said, "they will stop us and I don't have any motor insurance." Just as he said that, the police car turned its siren and blue lights on, instructing them to pull over. Andreas pulled over to the curb and stopped the car. One of the police officers got out of the car, leaving the driver behind the wheel on his police radio checking to see if the car was stolen.

"Is this your car?" asked the first policeman to Andreas, who was still in the driver's seat.

"Yes officer, it is." Andreas replied.

Bending his head through the window, checking out the three passengers, the police officer thought he could smell something.

"Are there any drugs in this car?" the officer asked.

"No sir" Andreas replied.

"Can you all step out of the car for one minute please?" asked the policeman.

The four cousins were now all standing in a line on the pavement; one officer was searching inside the car for drugs whilst the other asked the four for their names.

"Andreas Andrew" said the driver.

"Andrew Andrew" said the next. The police officer gave him a quizzical look then moved on to the third man.

"Andros Andrew" said the third. The officer hesitated then moved on to the fourth man asking him for his name.

"Andy Andrew" replied the fourth man.

"Are you being funny lads?" the policeman asked, "because wasting police time will get you all nicked. Now stop messing me about and give me your real names, or we will all take a trip to the local nick."

"They are our names, officer, we are all first cousins," Andreas Andrew said. "Andrew is our family name, and we are all named after our fathers first names."

At that point, the second officer got out of the car saying he had found nothing, so they let the boys go, because the paperwork was going to be too complex with the same name four times.

"Get on your way and don't get into any trouble."

SIX

Ratzilla was terrible at remembering names at the best of times but now that they all had the same name, it was going to be too complicated for him.

"Andrew" he called out loud.

"Which one boss?" the four shouted out in unison.

Right, this is going to get stupid, Ratzilla thought, as he studied their looks.

"You," as he pointed to Andros, "are tall Andrew."

"You," pointing to Andy, "are short Andrew."

"You," pointing to Andrew, "are Slim."

"And you," pointing to Andreas, "are Fat."

"I'm not fat," replied Andreas, "I just have a bit of a belly."

"Well, lose weight then if you don't want to be called fat", replied Ratzilla.

"Tall Andrew and Short Andrew, the first thing you must do is to bring Professor Giles Norton here. This is where he works." He handed them a small piece of paper. "You can read, I hope?"

"Slim and Fat Andrew, there are some old cells in the

basement, get one ready for our guest to stay in and then go and buy the following laboratory equipment." he said, handing them a large wad of money and a list.

"Well, what are you waiting for?!" yelled Ratzilla. Fail to plan, plan to fail, was his new favourite saying now. As the men went about their duties Ratzilla sat down in his big leather chair and stroked his cat.

"I think this suits me," he smiled to himself, just like all the big villains about to rule the world.

S E V E N

Ratzilla read the instructions that were on the computer disc over and over again. He had read them so many times he could quote them at will, but still he was not aware of their significance or their capability to destroy everyone in London. *Why would you let off a nerve gas in the heart of the City of London? How would that make you any money or were they terrorists who sent him the gun? Was this some kind of fancy robbery and he was the decoy?*

The only detail that Ratzilla did understand was that he had to get this Professor Norton and get him some equipment, so he could make this stuff that the people who sent him the gun required. If they were clever enough to make such a weapon, he wanted to be on their side. He did wonder though why they could not make their own gas, but soon dismissed this; *all this deep thought is not good for you.*

It wasn't long before Short Andrew and Tall Andrew returned, holding this man with what appeared to be a pillowcase over his head.

"Got him, boss," said Tall Andrew.

"Yeah, it's him alright. Professor Giles Norton," Short Andrew said.

"How can I be sure this is Norton?" said Ratzilla.

"Well, we asked at the university reception for Professor Norton, and we were directed to his office," Tall Andrew replied.

"The office door had Professor Norton written on it," Short Andrew said.

"And when we entered, we asked for Professor Norton and he said yes," added Tall Andrew.

"Does he have any ID on him?" Ratzilla asked. "What is this hanging round his neck?" Ratzilla observed.

Professor Giles Norton, Head of Organic Chemistry and Chemical Biology, University of London, and a photographed ID card. Ratzilla removed the pillowcase from his head and saw his mouth taped up to keep him quiet. It was definitely the same man as in the picture; *at least these two idiots could do something right,* he thought.

"Ah, Professor Norton. Welcome. You are probably wondering why I have had you brought here." Ratzilla said.

The professor was still unable to speak as he still had his mouth taped up.

"Remove the tape; this is no way to treat our guest." Ratzilla said.

"What the devil are you idiots doing with me? I shall go straight to the police and have you all arrested immediately!" The Professor shouted.

"I don't think so", Ratzilla said. "I have a small job for you to do and if you do it quickly and without fuss, I will let you live. If not, well, you work out the alternative." With that he gave Professor Norton something he had printed off the computer disc.

The professor quickly read through the instructions, gasped with horror, and looked up at Ratzilla.

"You will never get me or any sane person to make this for you. Where did you get these instructions from? You certainly don't have the brains to come up with this yourself."

"You will make this for me, Professor. Lock him in his cell!" Ratzilla shouted to Short Andrew and Tall Andrew.

"If you have the instructions, why do we need the Professor?" asked Short Andrew.

Ratzilla handed Short Andrew the instructions and saw his face flop like a confused child.

A few days in that dark damp cell will soften him up, Ratzilla thought.

One week later, Ratzilla was still no nearer to getting the Professor to do as the instructions wanted. He would have to get some sort of leverage to get the Professor to do his bidding.

Ratzilla summoned Tall Andrew and Short Andrew.

"I have a job for you," he said. "Go to the Professors house and see what you can find out about him that we can use to get him to do what we want."

Tall Andrew and Short Andrew returned a couple of hours later, dragging in a man again with a pillowcase around his head.

"You can't keep dragging in people with pillowcases around their head, especially in broad daylight, someone will see you!" Ratzilla bellowed. "Well, who is this?" demanded Ratzilla.

"It's the Professors son," Tall Andrew said smugly, knowing he had done something right for a change.

"The professor's son..." repeated Ratzilla, "Why didn't anyone tell me he had a son?

"You didn't ask us." said Short Andrew, "and anyway, he's only a young kid he can't help us.

"Remove that pillowcase. Let me see this young kid.", Ratzilla demanded.

"What's your name, boy?" asked Ratzilla, removing the pillowcase from his head, and at the same time removing the tape from the boy's mouth.

"Benedict Norton," replied the boy, "and I'm seventeen, soon to be eighteen. Who are you and why have you kidnapped me? My father doesn't have any money."

He paused for a moment, then asked "Do you know where my father is?"

"I'll ask the questions, boy," Ratzilla said. "Would you like to see your stubborn father, boy?" Ratzilla asked.

"What have you done with my father!" shouted Benedict.

"Still asking questions. You're as bad as your father," Ratzilla said. "Tie him to that chair and then bring his father here."

The professor was marched into the room. He looked very tired and thin. The professor was rubbing his eyes trying to get used to the light. He was not surprised to see his son there, he knew it would only be a matter of time before they would realise, he would not help them in any way, and find his son. He had come up with a plan to escape but hadn't had a chance to try it yet. If he could get them to untie Ben, he thought, they could both escape.

"I will not help you if you treat my son this way, untie him now," the professor demanded.

"There you go again, professor, demanding things. You do as we ask, and you and your son would be free to go. So, it's entirely up to you how long you are our guests," Ratzilla said, smugly.

"Did you get everything on the list I gave you?" Ratzilla asked.

"Yes, it's all waiting in your new lab," Slim Andrew replied.

"I want my son to assist me so I can get it done quicker and know he is alright," the professor demanded.

"I am glad you are starting to see sense, Professor. You can have your son assist you, but my men will be watching you at all times just in case you try anything clever," Ratzilla said.

EIGHT

"Are you alright, Benedict," said his father. "I'm sorry you have been dragged into this mess, but these idiots are planning something very scary, and we must try to stop them. Otherwise, London will be no more."

"Dad, you can't be planning on helping them if it's that bad, not for me," Ben replied.

"Stop all that whispering over there, or we will take the boy away," Short Andrew shouted.

"Trust me," said the Professor to his son, "just be ready to run when all hell breaks loose."

Night-time had drawn in and there was a vicious thunder and lightning storm raging outside; perfect cover to escape, the professor thought. He glanced over to his son who nodded to say he was ready.

The professor started to mix a couple of the ingredients, which quickly started to make a huge amount of smoke. It was not long before the whole room was covered in a thick fog.

"What's going on, Professor?" shouted Tall Andrew. "Quickly, go and get Ratzilla," he said to Short Andrew.

As the panic ensued, the professor and Ben got down on their knees and started to make for the door. Ratzilla was rushing towards the lab but before he could aim his laser gun at the two men, the professor jumped onto him, knocking him to the ground, the laser gun flying out of Ratzilla's hand. Ben ran through the door, into the derelict warehouse and out into the stormy night. Tall Andrew and Short Andrew had managed to wrestle the Professor to the ground whilst Ratzilla, picking up the gun, chased after Ben outside.

Ben jumped over a low wall into a small park and ran as fast as his legs would carry him into the darkness. As Ben was running across the open park, the night sky lit up with another flash of lightning. Ratzilla saw him and aimed his laser gun at him on the stun mode. As he squeezed the button, the sky lit up again and a lightning bolt appeared to strike Ben, at the same time as he was struck by the laser beam. There was an almighty bang and Ben collapsed to the ground. Fat Andrew and Slim Andrew were close behind Ratzilla.

"Quick! Get over the wall and bring the boy back to the warehouse. Even if he's dead we can't leave him, or the police will be all over the area." When Fat Andrew and Slim Andrew got to Ben, he had no vital signs.

"Is he dead?" asked Slim Andrew.

"Yes, I think so," said Fat Andrew.

They carried Ben's body back. Ratzilla checked for a pulse but found nothing, then told them to put the body in the other cell in the basement.

"Don't let the Professor know his son is dead. We can still use him as leverage," Ratzilla whispered.

"That was really stupid, Professor Norton. Someone could have got hurt. Your son will be kept away from you until you do as we want. Do I make myself clear?" Ratzilla demanded.

NINE

Ben slumped to the floor in front of Angus, grabbing at the big blue coat to cover his modesty.

"You just disappeared," Angus said, "right in front of my very own eyes."

"Come on mate, tell me how you did it. I won't tell anyone, I promise," said Angus.

"I don't know how it happens or why, but I was floating above your floor and the clothes just fell off me. Couldn't you see me?" Ben said.

"No, one minute you were there, then you just vanished, and your clothes just dropped to the floor," Angus said. "Right, let's just go through what happened and try to work it out." This was starting to be a real adventure, Angus thought all excitedly.

The two boys calmly repeated the conversation they had had word for word, but nothing happened.

"I can't figure it out," said Angus, "What was different about the first time that we are missing now?"

"I don't know, but you did make me angry laughing at me," Ben said.

"That's it!" said Angus. "You were angry. That must trigger something."

"But I was not angry in the cell or in the sewer, just scared. Very scared," Ben said.

"Right." Angus said, "What do being scared and angry have in common?"

"They are two separate emotions, they have nothing in common," Ben said angrily.

"Don't get angry with me, Ben, and *not* disappear. That is not helping at all," Angus snapped back.

"I'm very confused already. You are making things worse, Angus," pleaded Ben.

"Right, let's try getting you angry first and see what happens," Angus asked. "We can try scaring you later by putting a horror film on and watch it in the dark."

"I can't get angry just like that, I couldn't even get into the school play because my acting was awful. You will have to make me angry," Ben pleaded.

Angus thought for a moment, and then screamed as loud as he could.

"You're supposed to be making me angry, not deaf," shouted Ben.

Angus's bedroom was in the attic, accessed by wooden stairs. Both boys stared at each other, when they heard someone climbing the stairs to the attic room.

The door slowly swung open and standing there was Angus's mum, June.

"Who are you shouting at, Angus?" she enquired, looking round the room. "I thought I could hear shouting. You need to get out more, son, it's not good to talk to yourself, let alone *shout* at yourself."

"I was not shouting to myself, I was rehearsing my part in the school play," Angus replied. He tried to discreetly scan the room to see where Ben was without his mother suspecting anything, but he was nowhere to be seen. Ben must have disappeared again.

"You didn't say you were in the school play. What play is it, dear?" asked his mother, at the same time noticing a pile of ladies clothes on the floor. "Is that your costume dear", she asked pointing to the clothes dropped on the floor in the middle of the room.

"Romeo and Juliet," said Angus: the first play that came into his head. "And they are having a row, that's what I'm rehearsing." At the same time, he scooped up the clothes from the bedroom floor.

"I don't remember Romeo and Juliet rowing, is it a special version written by your teacher?" June asked. "Can you get some tickets for your father and I, please? We would love to see you on stage."

"Yes mum, can I please continue?" demanded Angus.

"Do you want me to read some lines with you, I love acting," June asked.

"No thanks mum, just some privacy please," Angus pleaded.

As June left the room and shut the door behind her, Angus was scurrying around the room looking for Ben.

Ben pulled himself from under the bed, trying to hide his modesty with his hands.

"How did you get under the bed?" Angus asked, at the same time handing Ben the discarded clothes.

"I hovered over when the door opened and slid under when you were talking to your Mum. I can't believe she didn't see me," Ben said, "I thought she was never going to go."

"One minute you were in my face, then you vanished again," Angus said.

"I'm still jumpy after last night. I thought those goons had found me; I was scared. I'm really worried. This is all freaking me out," Ben said. "And they still have my dad, I need to get help before they kill him. He won't make that nerve gas they want, never in a million years."

"I know, mate," Angus said, putting a hand on Ben's arm. "I know you are worried, and I'm going to try and help you, isn't that what mates are for?"

"We need to find out how and why you disappear before we go to the authorities or you will be locked up with the key thrown away," Angus said.

"What do you propose then? We do some experiments?" Ben said sarcastically.

"You might have something there, Ben," replied Angus. "Put these clothes on," Angus said abruptly, throwing Ben a pair of his jeans and a T-shirt he pulled out from his chest of drawers. "We are going out."

Ben is at least 3 inches taller than Angus, so both articles of clothing were far too short for him. He looked at himself in the mirror very indignantly and pulled a funny face. But before he could complain, Angus piped up. "You could always wear what you came here with."

After sneaking out, they decided to go to the local park, where Angus led them to some large children's climbing frames. Ben was never happy with heights and Angus knew it, so he thought this was a good place to start. Angus persuaded Ben to climb to the top of the largest point. He was a little nervous, nevertheless he gingerly reached the top of the frame trying very hard not to look down, but nothing happened. The boys decided after this failure to go to the local cinema and see the latest horror film, both hoping that being scared would induce Ben to disappear again. Whilst Ben and Angus were walking to the cinema down a quiet side-street, five boys came out from nowhere and surrounded Ben and Angus.

"Give us your money," they demanded, poking Angus in the stomach with something pointed. At the same time, another grabbed Ben round the neck from behind, pulling him back. "Ok, Ok," Angus shouted. Angus then instinctively tried to push the blade away from his stomach, but it would not budge.

At this point the five muggers shouted, "What the hell!" and started running away. Angus turned to see where his friend was, but there was only a pile of his clothes on the ground.

Angus instinctively reached down to the ground and gathered up the clothes. "Ben, where are you?" he said a couple of times, now drawing the attention of a couple of girls walking past that Angus knew.

"Hi," he said shyly, as the girls went past.

"Weirdo," was all Angus could make out as the girls went past, talking to themselves and giggling.

"Cheers, mate" Angus said out loud after the girls went past. "As if my love life was that great before, I'm going to be the laughingstock at the local girl's school now. Stop messing about Ben, where are you? If you don't come back immediately, I'm going home with the clothes."

Just then, Ben reappeared, again covering his modesty, quickly pulling the jeans on before anyone else came along.

"Can we just go back to your place, Angus? Please, I can't keep appearing naked in the middle of the street," Ben asked. "You think your love life is ruined? What chance will I have if it gets around I go streaking naked on the local high street?" Ben added.

"What are we going to do about those five muggers?" Angus asked. "We can't exactly go to the police. 'Well, officer,'" Angus continued, now mimicking an older man. "'The muggers, they just ran away when my friend disappeared. Yes officer, I did say disappear!'" Angus said in his own voice. "They would lock us both up."

The boys agreed to keep quiet about their lucky escape from the muggers and made their way back to Angus' home and the privacy of Angus' bedroom.

Ben went over all his emotions again and again for Angus, to see if they had missed something.

"What happens to you that then triggers you into disappearing?" Angus said out loud.

"If I knew that it would be a start at least," Ben said.

"So, what happens when you get scared?" Angus asked.

"I go a bit red and shake a bit," Ben replied.

"And what about when you got angry with me earlier," Angus reminded Ben.

"I got a bit hot in the face and started to shake," Ben said.

"So, what makes you shake?" Angus asked, "Think back to our biology GCSE."

"I hated biology so never did any more than pass my exams." Ben said.

"Well, aren't you lucky one of us paid attention in class," Angus said. "You go red because your blood pressure goes up, which also contributes to the shaking, I think."

"I must admit when I was escaping, my heart was beating so loud and fast I thought it was going to pop out of my chest," Ben explained. "That's also how I felt when that boy had me around the neck."

"And when Mum was walking up the stairs?" Angus asked, "How did you feel then?"

"I thought it was those goons and they had found me, so I got scared again," Ben said.

"Can you try and think about last night or today and the mugging and see if that works?" Angus asked.

Ben sat there concentrating very hard. He did go a bit red, but nothing happened.

"Try holding your breath for as long as you can," Angus suggested. "That makes me go red in the face."

"Really?" Ben replied "Is that all you can come up with."

"Just try," Angus said. "What have you got to lose by trying?"

Ben took in a deep breath and held it for as long as he could, which was quite a long time because Ben was very good at swimming under water. Ben started to go a bit crimson, then a bit darker still. Eventually he got so red that Angus thought he was going to explode. Angus leant over and took his friends wrist to check his pulse. He found it straight away; it was hammering through his skin. Then Angus was holding fresh air. Ben had vanished.

After a few seconds, Ben appeared behind the bed demanding Angus throw him his clothes.

"You are a genius, Angus!" Ben said. "At least now I can control it a bit better, although it took me over a minute to disappear."

Ben looked at his friend who was deep in thought for what seemed like an eternity, and then calmly spoke.

"Right then," said Angus, "When your heart beats fast you vanish, so that's why nobody can see you and your clothes fall off you. When your heartbeat goes back to normal you reappear. That all makes perfect sense now."

"Makes sense to you maybe," declared Ben, "but I am getting more and more freaked out by the minute."

"Wow, Ben, think about what you can do when you can control this a bit better!" remarked Angus, " you would be able to walk into the girls changing rooms at school and no one will see you, I'm so jealous!"

"You pervert, Angus, but this is really serious. Stop teasing me." Ben demanded. "And anyway, the first place I'm going is the teacher's staffroom. I want to hear all the gossip about us."

"What about the teachers gossiping about the teachers?" Angus said, "That would be even juicier. But first you need to work out how to get your heart racing when you want, and not take over a minute each time," Angus said. "The clothes issue, or lack of clothes, might take a little longer to resolve, but your dad could help there…Your dad! We need to come up with a plan on rescuing him. Or go to the police and tell them everything. They might believe you before they lock you up in a mental institution."

"How will I find him? I was walking for hours. All I know is that they are north of the Thames," said Ben

Angus started to pace up and down his room again with the pen back in his mouth.

"Go home," shouted Angus.

"Thanks, mate, for your help and support, you're now kicking me out? Some friend you are!" Ben shouted.

"Quiet, or Mum will really suspect something is up. No, I mean go home and they will come to you," Angus replied. "They found you there before; they are not very bright you say, so they might think you will go home again to get clothes or something."

"Getting caught again, how will that help my father, clever dick?" Ben said.

"They can't catch you; don't you see? You can vanish at will. Well, not yet you can't, but we can practice," Angus said.

"Of course! I understand now. I'll let them take me back to my father, escape and set him free, then we can go to the police. We don't have to tell the police everything, do we Angus? It's all clear now," Ben said.

"Right," said Angus, "let's see how we can get you to control your heartbeat faster. Holding your breath is too slow. You must be able to do it at will and maintain it for as long as you need. What about Sarah? You've always fancied her. Think of you and her together, you know."

"You are such a pervert, Angus, a one-track mind," said Ben.

"I'm a healthy, 17-year-old young man; there is nothing wrong with thinking about girls, or boys if you prefer that," Angus replied.

"I can't help thinking about Dad," Ben said, "and what they are trying to make him create. This nerve gas and what they intend to use it for, it makes me so angry."

At this, Ben disappeared again.

"That's it!" shouted Angus, unable to control himself.

"You've done it again!" He then proceeded to jump up and down, yelling, "We've done it again!"

"What is going on up there, Angus?" shouted his mother from the bottom of the stairs.

"Nothing Mum, sorry. I'll keep it down," Angus replied. "How am I going to explain about the school play now as well?"

Ben appeared again, scrambling for some cover.

"With some practice, I think I can do it at will," Ben said. "Do you want me to have a word with your mum? I can smooth things over for you. She's always liked me."

"And how are you going to do that Ben?" Angus asked.

"'Mrs. Sinclair? It was me in Angus's room; I was just practising my new skill of disappearing. Would you like me to demonstrate? Oh, and by the way, to save you from blushing, when I reappear, I am going to be completely naked.'" Angus said, mimicking his friend's voice.

"No, not quite Angus," Ben said. "I would just tell her it was me up here all along."

"For a clever kid, you're not very bright, Ben, are you?" Angus stated. "Why were you hiding? No, leave it to me. I can handle my mum. I'll just say the part in the play was beneath me, and I don't want to do it anymore," Angus continued.

Ben thanked Angus for all his help, and said that he was the best friend ever, and would keep in touch over the next few days. Ben then set off home, hoping they were waiting for him there. This thought started to make him nervous, but he fought to control his nerves, or he would disappear and be naked again in public. On arriving home, he stopped on the opposite corner to his house, and it all looked quiet. Were they really that dumb and waiting for him? Because he could be bringing the police. Or was he the dumb one, walking into a trap. *There's only one way to find out,* he thought, as he crossed the road. The thought of saving his father from these monsters would keep him strong, and anyway, the good guys always win. Don't they?

"If I die, I will come back and haunt you, Angus, for suggesting this," he said out loud.

TEN

Ben sneaked round the back of his house and climbed up the back, using the extension roof, into his bedroom window. He always kept it unlocked because he was always losing his keys and dad would moan about having to get another key cut.

"We might as well have a spare key at the key-cutters," his dad would complain, and the last six times threatened to take it out of his allowance, but never did.

Dad was a big softy, Ben thought. *He can't make a nerve gas; he would rather die than make anything that could kill people. I've got to help him.*

Ben took a shower and packed a small bag with spare clothes. He was starting to think more clearly now, and knew that if they were not here by now waiting for him, he would have to go to North London and find them himself. *Why did I not make a note of where I was when I escaped?* he thought to himself. *Because I was scared and had other things on my mind,* he reminded himself. Arguing with himself was not going to get his father back, he thought.

I will have to back track from Albert Bridge and see what becomes familiar. London is such a big city; this will take forever.

Once he arrived at the bridge, he hid his bag in the bushes by the riverbank and started to walk north, but he could not remember which way he had come to the river.

I know, he thought, *I will make myself invisible and fly over the roof tops until I see something familiar. Yep, that sounds like a plan,* he thought. He started to make himself angry and held his breath, just like he had practiced at home, and it worked! He shed his clothes and started to float up to the rooftops. This made him really scared, so it was really easy to keep his heart racing.

Right now, Ben was thinking: *How do I get moving forward and steer my body? This is not as simple as it is made to look in the movies.* He started to flail his arms in a forward motion and made a walking movement. This worked, but very slowly. *Maybe if I put myself in a diving position, this would propel me quicker.* He did look like superman, but was not going very fast at all, and could walk quicker on the ground. Then it came to him; *I will find the tallest building and run off the roof! That will give me some speed.*

Ben started to look around. The first thing he saw that might work was the derelict Battersea Power station, but it would take him forever to get that high, and there didn't appear to be anything flat enough for him to get a good running jump. Just by Vauxhall bridge are a number of large apartment blocks. *I'll use one of them. After all, what could go wrong? I can't die...or can I?"* he hesitated.

The block next to the bridge had no lights on in the penthouse flat, so he chose that one. It took a few minutes, but he managed to flail his way to the top floor and landed on the roof.

After calming himself down, he reappeared naked as usual. *I hope this works,* he thought, *or I'm going for a swim in the Thames.* He didn't need to try very hard to get his pulse racing. He was scared, so scared he started to jog, then got faster and faster. All the time the edge of the building was getting closer and closer. Ben started to have doubts. *What am I doing?* he said to himself as the edge appeared before him. About a metre from the edge, he disappeared. He had the momentum now and flew off the roof at quite a speed and was travelling towards North London.

London from up here looked completely different. He was flying like a bird. *This is great!* Ben thought. After a few minutes, Ben went over Buckingham Palace. *I wonder if the Queen is in,* he thought. *I could fly past her windows! No, that would make me into a peeping Tom,* he thought. Ben veered right towards Piccadilly Circus and then up Shaftesbury Avenue. These places he knew because he loved the theatre so much. It was the only thing he and his father did together anymore.

It came to Ben that he had not walked through the West End of London last night, *so it must have been further over towards Hyde Park,* he thought. As he swept over the park, he started to enjoy this freedom of flying more and more. Then suddenly, he started to plummet towards the ground, falling like a stone. *I'm going to die now! If I'm not dead already, I soon will be!* He was falling at a great speed and had no parachute, not that he knew how to use one anyway, and Ben was sure he was far too low for a parachute to work. Just as suddenly, he started to float again. *Phew, that was too close for comfort, and very scary.* Thankfully, because that's what saved his life (if he *is* still alive.)

Of course, he thought, *I was enjoying flying so much that my heart rate slowed down, that's when I started to fall. So, when I thought I was going to die, it started to race again. This is so fantastic! I hope nobody saw me, that would definitely make the morning papers.*

I can see the headlines now. UFO seen flying over central London. Is it a bird, is it a plane? No, it's a naked boy flying down to earth without a parachute! There'll be a few drunks quitting the drink tonight! Ben thought, laughing out loud.

Or maybe an alien attack, yes, that's more likely, 'Alien vanishes over London sky'. The headline writers will have a field day.

What if someone filmed it on their phone? It could go viral, and then I would be famous, and naked, for the whole world to see. You can't do anything in London today without getting caught on camera.

Let's worry about social media, the papers and television stations tomorrow, Ben decided, and continued North in search of Ratzilla and rescuing his father.

Thinking of how to land started to scare him again. *I'll work it out,* he tried to convince himself. *What's the worst thing that can happen to him now after all he's been through?*

ELEVEN

Lizzie Summer, a tall beautiful twenty-year-old, was the top in her class at school. She was destined to follow both her parents to Oxford but instead she was working for MI6. Headhunted at seventeen, she was promised all the opportunities that working for her government's secret service would bring her. These could not be matched by any other career.

Lizzie had a very unique skill. She could glance at an image or photograph and recall it along with all its details. Working in the MI6 observation suite in Vauxhall, Lizzie longed to go out into the field and do some real work for her country, but her boss Robert Jenkins-Smyth just kept on saying to her "to be patient."

"You're still in training," he would remind her, but patience was not Lizzie's strong point.

It was just going to be another routine morning at work, Lizzie thought: going over hundreds of pictures, looking for anything suspicious or anybody on the growing wanted list. As she walked into the office, all her colleagues were huddled over one screen, looking at something over and over again.

"What's all the fuss about?" said Lizzie, walking up to

the computer screen surrounded by her colleagues.

"Look at this, see what you think, Lizzie." said Bertrand, one of her colleagues and fiercest rivals for any promotions. "What do you make of this?"

Lizzie leant over to look at this five second piece of action taken from one of the rooftop cameras at MI6 headquarters at Vauxhall. It appeared to show a naked young man jump off the roof of the apartment block just the other side of the bridge and disappear in thin air.

"The camera has been checked," said Bertrand, "and has not been tampered with."

This is a prank, thought Lizzie, *I better be careful what I say. These guys are always looking for ways to put me down because they know I'm much cleverer than any of them.*

"Who checked that this is all correct and accurate?" said Lizzie.

"I did," said Brian, "I have checked and double checked everything, and I was thinking this is either a prank or some TV set up. But it appears not, Lizzie." Brian was the most senior and experienced officer in their department and known for his no-nonsense approach. Not one to play pranks, far from it.

"We have all been ordered to drop what we are doing and get to the bottom of this. That comes direct from number 10, the PM himself."

Lizzie sat at her station and watched the film once more to make sure. She knew that face and would be the first to identify him. Of that, she was sure. *The Prime minister is aware of this,* Lizzie thought, *this could be my opportunity to get recognised and even promoted.* Lizzie went online and immediately found what she was looking for, a science monthly from last month. Lizzie clicked through the pages and found an article by Professor Norton, and as she thought, it contained a picture of the Professor and his son.

"That's him!" she said out loud. The whole team came rushing over to her station.

"How the hell did you find him so quick?" demanded Bertrand.

"Intuition, some people call it. You either have it or not," Lizzie replied, grinning from ear to ear because she had just beaten Bertrand to solving this very important problem, and he would be livid.

"We need to get this to field operations immediately and pick Professor Norton and his son up," said Brian.

"May not be that simple," said Lizzie, "the professor has not been to work for a couple of weeks according to an article in last night's paper. He may have developed something and is using his son to test it on."

"What has the professor invented?" Bertrand asked. "The ability to fly unaided, the ability to vanish, or maybe both." There was a chuckle of laughter around the office.

The laughter stopped the moment Robert Jenkins-Smyth entered the office. He was the head of MI6 and not someone renowned for his sense of humour. Jenkins-Smyth was a heavily decorated SAS officer and had joined the secret service after he had been wounded on an undercover operation in the Middle East. Not known for being hands on meant to everyone present that this was of the utmost importance if he was taking an active role.

"Let's just find them both first before we jump to any conclusions," Brian demanded, after getting the nod to proceed from Jenkins-Smyth.

TWELVE

After flying around over North London for a couple of hours, Ben was getting very tired. Keeping your heart racing was not as easy as he thought and was making him very hungry.

Ben decided to go back home and try again the following night. He made his way back to Albert Bridge where he had hidden his spare clothes. He was approaching the bridge at quite a speed which was making him very scared again. *Right,* he thought, *I will make a nice gentle landing by those bushes.* He started to flail his arms and legs as if to slow himself down, but he was still travelling too fast.

Why didn't I think about the landing? I'll meditate, that's what I'll do. He managed to get himself to fly round in a small circle above the bushes then he attempted to calm himself down by trying to meditate. This would have been easier if he had ever meditated before, but he thought it was all rubbish. He needs to open up a bit more and not be so dismissive of other people and their beliefs.

Right, he thought, *breathe slowly, close your eyes and start counting sheep, that use to help him sleep when he was younger.*

Ouch, he thought, *these bushes are scratching me on my bare bottom! I'm back. Where is my bag?* He scrambled to get dressed before anyone spotted him. Surprisingly for London, his discarded clothes were also still there, so he packed them in his bag before anyone noticed him in the bushes.

I'll go home and eat, then rest before tonight then try again, he thought.

When Ben got to his house, he went straight round to the back, not noticing the two cars parked across the road with blacked out windows.

Then, Ben climbed up to the extension roof and into his bedroom window.

I need some food, he thought, *I'm starving; this flying gives you such an appetite.*

Next thing he felt a jab on his neck, and then darkness again.

Opening his eyes, Ben felt groggy and was still very hungry. He could see a number of strange faces staring at him, but they didn't seem menacing like the goons who had his father; They wore suits and looked more like police. He was not in his bedroom either, it looked like an interrogation room (not that he had ever been in one before, but he had seen them in films). One wall was a mirror from floor to ceiling.

A one-way mirror, he thought. *They must be watching me from behind there also. I must keep calm and not let them see me disappear until I find out what is going on, and this time make a note of where I am.*

"Who are you?" Ben demanded. "Where am I?"

"The boys starting to come round," one of the suits said into a phone.

Ben sat in this chair with both his hands and legs strapped down. Nobody said a word to him for a couple of minutes. Then the door swung open, and two men entered the room followed by this heavenly goddess of a young woman. They all huddled round and whispered amongst themselves. Then everyone except one man walked out of the room.

"Where is your father?" the man asked in a quiet but aggressive way. He was tall straight backed, very military like in his manner.

"I don't know" Ben replied.

"Let's start again. My name is Cameron Scott and I work for Her Majesties government, MI6 to be precise, and we need to find your father urgently." This time his voice was much softer and calmer.

"I really don't know", Ben said "I've been looking for him myself. Why am I tied up? I haven't done anything wrong."

"I want to show you a short film and I want you to explain what happened," Cameron said. "Then we will help you to find your father.

Ben watched the five second clip of him jumping off the apartment block at Vauxhall and disappearing.

"Please can you explain this for me?" Cameron asked.

Ben was not sure whether to explain everything, hold some details back (like him being able to disappear at will) but decided if they were from MI6 then they could help him get his father back safe and sound. If not, he would just disappear and leave.

"Well, it all started when I woke up in this dark cell." Ben started telling this man and everyone else the other side of the mirror the whole story to date.

Cameron listened patiently to Ben's version of events. Ben was at last glad to be telling someone who might believe him. If the queen's government and secret service didn't believe him, then nobody would.

"And then I woke up here," Ben said.

"So, you can disappear and fly through walls?" Cameron said, smugly. "Really, you want me to believe this far-fetched story? Your father has invented something that can make you invisible is really the truth, stop covering for him Ben. We will get the truth out of you one way or another. So, you might as well tell us the truth now and save us all a lot of time.

"I am telling the truth," Ben insisted. "I know it sounds far-fetched but it's the truth, please believe me."

"Well, if you want us to believe you, can you give us a demonstration please?" Cameron asked.

Ben had managed to keep himself calm throughout the interrogation but there was something believable about this whole set up. They did seem to work for the government. If not, he would soon find out. If they were government security, then they would be able to find his father a lot easier than he would by himself and stop that evil Ratzilla from attacking London with a nerve gas.

Ben started to make his pulse race and after a few seconds his clothes dropped to the floor and he was floating in the room. Ben was quite pleased with himself. He was getting better and better at controlling this.

All hell broke loose as a stream of suits, and that gorgeous young lady, came filing back into the room, everyone staring down at the small pile of discarded clothes and then at each other, questioning what they had just witnessed.

"Ok Ben, that was quite impressive," shouted Cameron. "You can come back now, we believe you."

"Clear the room so he can come back and get dressed," a voice said.

Ben being the nosy type drifted through the mirror to see who was watching. He was not prepared for what he saw. There were at least five people dressed like doctors as well as half a dozen suits. *Probably MI6, he thought.* One of the doctors was preparing a syringe. *Was that for me? he thought. That's how they must have got me here before. They drugged me. They won't let me go, I'm too valuable.* Ben then found himself staring at the young lady. *She is the most beautiful girl I've ever seen,* he thought. *When this is all over, I'm going to ask her out on a date. But first things first, we need to find my father.*

Whatever happens, thought Ben, *I must not let them get behind me so they can use that needle on me.*

"Come on Ben," pleaded Cameron, "You've proven your point. We want to help you find your father."

Ben appeared by the chair where he was strapped and grabbed his clothes to cover himself up.

"Ah good," said Cameron, "Welcome back. We're not going to hurt you, I promise. We want to help."

"You couldn't hurt me even if you wanted to," Ben replied. "And you can keep that man with the big needle away from me or you won't see me again," he demanded.

There was chattering behind the mirror. "He must have been in here and seen us," Robert Jenkins-Smyth said. "We can't let him escape. That's why they have his father, they want Ben and what he can do for their terrorist cause."

"But he said they wanted his father to make a nerve gas," Lizzie interrupted.

"Of course. He won't tell us his father invented this, so he made up the story about the two flashes of light," Bertrand responded.

"Imagine if you had people that could disappear at will, or better still, an army of soldiers that can disappear and reappear at will," Jenkins-Smyth continued. "You would rule the world. What would Her Majesties government do to prevent this falling into enemy hands? Or even better still, what could we do with this ourselves?"

"What if terrorists had this ability? Nobody would be safe," Bertrand said. "This is far bigger than any of us thought."

"I must call a meeting of the Security Council. Send me a copy of the boy disappearing here today, and I don't need to remind anyone, this is top, top secret. Just keep him here. Is that clear?" demanded Jenkins-Smyth. "He must not be allowed to leave."

"Have you seen the way he looked at you, Lizzie?" said Bertrand. "He's really smitten with you."

"Don't be silly," said Lizzie, blushing slightly. "I'm the only female here that's why he smiled at me, no other reason."

"We could use that to our advantage," said Bertrand. "He's only a young boy, and if he has a crush on you…"

"You want me to be friendly with him just to keep tabs on him?" Lizzie replied.

"If Ben likes you, that would be useful," Brian said, interrupting their conversation.

"Well, you have always said you wanted a field post. This could not be a bigger opportunity for you to do just that," Bertrand said.

Brian proceeded to call Cameron Scott into the anti-room and inform him of what had just been discussed.

"That can't do any harm, even if it keeps the boy calm and stops him from trying to escape," Cameron said. "Ok young lady, you go and get to know Ben while we try and locate his father."

Lizzie was fuming as she made her way into the interrogation room. "Young lady indeed," Lizzie said under her breath. "That's all they think I'm good for, just looking pretty, eye candy. I'll show them how good an operative I am."

With a false smile on her face, she entered the room where Ben was. He was now dressed again and not tied to the chair but standing in the far corner of the room, as far away as he could be from the door and mirror.

He doesn't trust us, Lizzie thought, *and I don't blame him. By the time the scientists have finished with him he'll be getting his old age pension.*

"Hi, my name is Lizzie," she said as she walked towards the corner Ben was standing in.

He went bright red and struggled to reply. "My name's Benedict, Ben to my friends. But you know that don't you. Do you work for the government, Lizzie?" enquired Ben. *What a lame response,* he thought to himself. *It's up there with 'Do you come here often.'*

"You seem a very nice kid" Lizzie said.

"Nice kid?" Ben interrupted, "I'll be eighteen soon."

"Sorry," Lizzie said. "I'm here to help you. I'm not the enemy."

"You make sure nobody comes near me with a needle," Ben demanded. "Then I will help you as much as I can to get my father back."

"That's a deal." replied Lizzie. "When you recounted your story to Cameron, was anything left out about your father's research? Could they be after him for some other reason?"

"No." said Ben. "My father would never make anything that would harm anybody. He would rather die. They want him to make a nerve gas that will kill thousands of people."

"So, you being able to disappear was an accident then, Ben?" enquired Lizzie.

"Yes. All I can remember is running through this small park, seeing two flashes of light, and waking up in this dark damp cell," Ben replied.

"What about when you came out of the sewer? Do you remember anything about where you were then?" Lizzie asked. "Close your eyes and think back."

"I will help you, but you must clear the room first. I don't trust these suits; they might drug me again," Ben demanded.

"Ok, everyone out please! Ben wants to talk to me alone!" Lizzie shouted.

There was a lot of grumbling noises of disapproval, but they all did as Lizzie requested. She did hear one sentence that was clear enough for her to understand: "Who does she think she is ordering us about?" Probably Bertrand, Lizzie thought.

The room soon cleared, and they were now alone, apart from everyone watching through the full-length mirror. It was like being alone but in front of a television camera. Who knows how many people were watching?

"Ok Ben," said Lizzie, "close your eyes and think about what you saw when you came up from the sewer".

"There were two people at a bus stop opposite. They looked like a couple," Ben said. "I thought it was strange that they didn't see me, especially as I was naked and floating in mid-air. But their bus came straight away, and they got on board."

"Could you see what the number of the bus was?" Lizzie asked.

"No, I couldn't see the number, only the side of the bus," Ben replied.

Ben carried on for a few minutes while Lizzie kept asking him to keep his eyes closed and see if he could recall anything: a name of a road or station.

"No, I can't think of anything that would give me a location," Ben kept saying. "My head was pounding; I was confused and then…" Ben hesitated.

"And? And what?" said Lizzie.

"I even thought about going to the hospital, but it was a community hospital, and I didn't know what that meant. I thought they might lock me up for being mad or something."

"Can you remember what it was called, this community hospital you saw?" Lizzie asked.

"I'm trying. I'm trying to think."

Lizzie got out her phone and started to type when Ben shouted: "Paddington! Paddington Community Hospital. That's it. If we go there, I might find where my father is."

Before Ben had even finished speaking, the suits came marching back in the room. They had of course been listening to everything.

"Well done, Lizzie" said Cameron Scott, "we'll take over from here."

"But Sir, I want to accompany Ben to help find his father."

"You're not trained for field duties, Lizzie. We will take over now," Cameron demanded. "Well done young lady. Your part in this will not go unrecognised, I can assure you of that. Ok Ben, you will accompany us to West London, and we will try to locate your father. But any disappearing could put your father's life in danger. You are now officially helping her Majesties' government in avoiding a terrorist attack on London. Do I make myself clear?"

THIRTEEN

Fat Andrew came storming into the Lab where Ratzilla was looking at all the equipment still unused. Professor Norton was still refusing to co-operate even with the threat of his son being killed.

"What is it now? Have you done what I asked?" Ratzilla demanded.

"I have to speak to you, boss" replied Fat Andrew.

"Tall Andrew! Short Andrew!" Ratzilla shouted. "Take Professor Norton back to his cell."

Ratzilla followed Fat Andrew out of the lab, but not before he turned to the professor and reminded him of the conversation they had had earlier.

"Two more hours, Professor, or your son will be killed."

Ratzilla waited until the professor was out of ear shot and well on his way back to his cell, then turned to Fat Andrew.

"Well, where is the boy?" demanded Ratzilla. "Don't tell me you have returned without him."

"We were waiting at the boys' house for hours," Fat Andrew said.

"Well, what do you want? Overtime?" Ratzilla remarked.

"Do we get overtime?" Fat Andrew asked. After a short pause he continued, thinking that the boss was joking about the overtime. "We were hungry boss, so we went to get some food," Fat Andrew continued.

"Who went to get some food?" Ratzilla interrupted.

"We all went," Fat Andrew said.

"You all went to get some food!" screamed Ratzilla. "Did you not think that one of you should stay and keep an eye out?"

"Well, we didn't know what we wanted to eat," Fat Andrew said.

"We all had kebab in the end," Short Andrew interrupted, as he entered the room accompanied by Tall Andrew. "The professor is all snug in his cell," he said smugly.

"I'm so pleased you managed to get something to eat, I wouldn't want you boys getting hungry, it's not as if this is very important is it!?" Ratzilla said his voice getting louder and louder.

"When we returned to the boy's home we noticed, parked across the road from the professor's house, two cars with blacked out windows and some men inside each," Fat Andrew continued. "They did look very suspicious, so we hid and waited. Then a little while later we saw the boy. He looked like he was unconscious and was being carried out by another two men in suits and put into the back of one of the cars."

"You'll never guess where they took the boy, boss." Tall Andrew said. Tall Andrew thought he should be rewarded for this piece of information. "MI6 headquarters at Vauxhall. We know its MI6 because it was blown up in a James Bond film we saw."

"Blown up in a Bond film…" Ratzilla repeated, just in case he was hearing things or really going crazy.

"Yes boss, it's the film where Daniel Craig was Bond; they blow out the back of the building using M's laptop." Tall Andrew continued.

"No, it's the one where the money is covered with explosive stuff Pierce Brosnan was in," Short Andrew interrupted.

"When you two finish your debate on Bond films…" Ratzilla said trying very hard to remain calm. "So, you followed them to MI6 and did what?" Ratzilla continued.

"We sat in a café across the road and waited," Fat Andrew said.

"We were still hungry," Tall Andrew said. "Those kebabs in South London were nice but very small, in North London you get much bigger portions."

"Will you stop talking about food you idiots," Ratzilla shouted. "Are you sure you were not followed back here? Tall Andrew, go and check outside and keep a look out." Ratzilla demanded. He knew that these idiots would bring MI6 back for sure. *I'm getting the gun and getting out,* Ratzilla thought. *If they get the professor, so be it, but they won't get me if I can help it.*

"Why would MI6 get involved?" Ratzilla started to think out loud. "If the boy went to the authorities, they would not stake out his house, then carry him off unconscious. Unless they are onto us because of this," Ratzilla raised the gun in front of him. "Or they have the people who sent this and know what they are up to."

"What do you want us to do?" said Short Andrew.

"Start packing everything in the lab up, we will have to

move somewhere else." Ratzilla said. He then proceeded to unstun Slim Andrew as he knew they needed all the help they could get if MI6 was on their trail.

Ratzilla had decided to slip away quietly and let these four idiots take the blame; they only knew his name as Ratzilla so he could easily set up somewhere else. As long as he had the gun, he could make lots of money and hide from the people who sent it to him. "I'll be fine" he kept on trying to reassure himself, "I'm not frightened of MI6."

Ratzilla turned to walk out the door when three men came bursting in. His instinct to keep himself alive kicked in and he fired the gun at the three without even checking to see what the gun was set on. During the following commotion he managed to get to the basement door and went down to the sewers where he thought he could escape whoever was attacking them. This day was inevitable, so he had planted a bag with his getaway gear; Well, it was just full of money he had stashed away, his passport and a change of underwear.

FOURTEEN

Ben sat in the back of a large car with blacked out windows and officers on either side of him. The car was one of a convoy of five vehicles, and they were in the middle one. This made Ben feel really important but still a little nervous. Ben kept thinking about the way they kidnapped him from his house, and yes, they are trying to locate his father, but only because they think the professor has developed some kind of weapon that would give them a huge advantage in global dominance.

A message came over the radio in the car:

"Target location confirmed, proceed to Maida Vale."

"What's going on?" Ben asked.

Robert Jenkins-Smyth who was sitting in the front seat turned to answer Ben.

"When we picked you up from your house earlier today, there were three men watching your house," Robert said.

"They also followed us back to HQ," he continued. "But what they didn't know was we had spotted them and were now watching their every move. The three then led us back to an old warehouse in Maida Vale. It has a park nearby that fits the description you gave us, so it all looks quite promising."

When the convoy arrived, Ben had to stay in the car with his two minders.

"I can help you before you go in. I know the layout and can go in without anybody seeing me," Ben pleaded with Jenkins-Smyth.

Reluctantly Robert Jenkins-Smyth agreed as it would not put his men at risk and ensure they could locate the professor and extract him safely.

"Ok, Ben. You have five minutes to go in and locate all the gang and your father. You will come straight out and leave the rest to us. No heroics, it's the only way if you want to see your father again alive. Do I make myself clear?" demanded Jenkins-Smyth.

"Yes," Ben replied, "I know what I have to do, don't worry. They can't hurt me."

It's your father we want safe, Jenkins-Smyth thought, *Ben was useful, but Professor Norton was irreplaceable if he had invented the ability to disappear.*

Ben proceeded to disappear and enter the warehouse, at first stepping quietly past Tall Andrew. Then inside, he located Ratzilla who was deep in thought but had the gun in his hand, and saw the others gathering up all the equipment from the lab. Ben then made his way down to the cells where he found his father. He was so tempted to reappear and hug his father, but he was going to do as he was told. He made his way back to the convoy of MI6 vehicles and briefed everyone on the location of all the gang and his father.

"Very well done, Ben," Jenkins-Smyth said. "Now leave the rest to us."

Ben watched as the secret service started to attack in deftly silence. First, they took out Tall Andrew, capturing him alive and then entered the building. Suddenly and completely unexpectedly there was a series of flashes followed by gun fire. *This was not going to plan,* Ben thought. He tried to get out of the car he was in but the two men protecting him said he should stay put as all was under control. How they could know that was beyond him, but before he could respond he saw Robert Jenkins-Smyth leaving the warehouse and coming towards them.

"Follow me, Ben, but be quiet and very careful." On entering, Ben noticed three MI6 operatives frozen like statues, but they looked totally unharmed. No bullet wounds or blood.

"Can you explain any of this?" demanded Robert. "What has happened to my men? Are they dead or what?"

"No, I'm sorry but I can't," Ben said.

Robert Jenkins-Smyth turned to one of his men and started barking out instructions. "I want this whole area cordoned off and forensics brought in to check all these bodies. Call in the medics. I want to know if they are dead or alive. Ben, three of my men have been shot or stunned but are not dead; well, I don't think they are. Can you identify the gang and tell me which one is Ratzilla? Ben scoured the floor where the bodies of Fat Andrew, Slim Andrew and Short Andrew lay.

"He's not here," Ben said. "He must have used the gun on your men and escaped with it."

Ben asked if they had checked the cells in the basement.

"No not yet," came a reply. "My men are about to go down now and get your father. You can take them if you want but be very careful, we still haven't found this Ratzilla fellow yet." Ben proceeded to lead the way down to the cells in the basement with two armed men closely following.

It didn't take long to locate the cells, and the keys were conveniently hanging on a hook outside the first door. The security team told Ben to stand to one side as they drew their guns from their holsters. Ben tried to tell them that was not necessary, but they didn't listen.

"It's ok, kid, we know what we are doing." Slowly they unlocked the door and looked inside. It was empty.

"I tried to tell you," insisted Ben, "He's in the second cell and you don't need guns. He's unarmed and alone."

"But we don't know where that Ratzilla chap is, so please keep quiet and let us handle it," replied one of the MI6 men.

They then proceeded to unlock the second cell door and again with guns drawn they entered the cell. As soon as the first officer entered, a cloud of dirt came flying in their direction, hitting them square in the face. Then this man charged at the security men, screaming like a mad man, shoving them both to the ground, then scrambling out of the door. He tried to lock the door, but before he could, he heard his son's voice.

"Dad its ok! It's me Ben. I've come to rescue you! These men work for the government."

The professor turned to see his son standing there.

"You're OK, Ben," Professor Norton said as he hugged his son so tight Ben thought he was going to suffocate. "I thought you were dead; I overheard those clowns say you were dead. I'm so sorry gentlemen," as the professor tried to dust the two officers down with his bare hands, making their suits even dirtier. "I heard the gunfire and didn't know what was going on," said the professor,

"I'm sort of fine, Dad" Ben said.

"Sort of, what do you mean sort of?" The professor pushed Ben away a little and strained in the gloom to look his son over. "You look fine to me, Ben." the professor replied.

"It's a very long story, Dad, but this is not over yet," Ben explained to his father, as they made their way back upstairs. Ben was trying to update his father about the gang and Ratzilla's escape, when he was interrupted by Jenkins Smyth.

"Ah Professor Norton, my name is Robert Jenkins Smyth and I head this unit. I'm so glad to see you looking well. Did they harm you at all Professor Norton?"

Robert put his arm around the professor and walked him away so nobody could hear what he was saying. "We have bodies of the gang, Professor, and three of my best men stunned and in a state of limbo," said Robert, "and a hell of a lot of unanswered questions. We're going to take you and your son somewhere safe so you can help us get to the bottom of all of this." Robert called for some men to take Ben and his father back to Vauxhall to be debriefed.

On the journey back, Ben proceeded to update his father about the new skills he had acquired since the night of their failed escape. What they didn't know was their whole conversation was being recorded. They were still being held, but by a different gang.

Back at the warehouse it did not take long before the whole place was swarming with people in white forensic suits, going over everything with meticulous care. The three stunned MI6 officers had been taken by ambulances to a secret government medical centre so tests could be carried out, and hopefully to bring them out of this coma type state they were in. Robert Jenkins-Smyth was back at MI6 HQ with Professor Norton and Ben, going over their statements line by line to see if any of this made any sense.

FIFTEEN

Ben and the Professor were summoned to a large boardroom. Seated around the table was Lizzie Summer. Ben smiled when he saw her. Also, there was Lizzie's colleagues, Bertrand, and Brian. Ben scanned the room; there were a number of people in military uniforms of all types, very senior by the number of medals they had. Also, a very official looking man at the head of the table with Robert Jenkins-Smyth at his side.

The man at the head of the table welcomed Ben and his father to the meeting.

"Now that our two guests have joined us, I will let Robert Jenkins-Smyth bring you all up to date."

Robert Jenkins-Smyth stood up and turned to his left.

"Thank you, Home Secretary Adams. "Now that we have finished analysing the computer we found at the warehouse, continued Robert Jenkins-Smyth, "it is clear that James Ratsby, alias Ratzilla, was sent the gun and instructions. This we know because of the comprehensive instructions contained in the disc we found with the computer. The computer that was found at the warehouse contains information about this mysterious weapon. In fact, it contained not only instructions for its set up and use but also what they wanted Ratzilla to do as payment for the gun. It had details on the Professor and the nerve gas that they wanted him to make, and where he was going to use it. We can also conclude from our debriefing of Professor Norton and his son Ben, that Ratzilla never met the people he was working for. We have also deduced that our three officers have been stunned and can be revived once we have Ratzilla in custody with his gun. It is also apparent that only he can use this weapon. Unfortunately, we do not know who made this gun and where it came from or any of the technology behind it, but we are convinced it is a terrorist threat from abroad. Professor Norton has given us a list of all other chemists capable of making this nerve gas. We have them all under surveillance in case Ratzilla makes contact."

"With regard to Ben and his special powers, we have concluded that this was caused by him being shot with this gun and being struck by lightning at precisely the same time. We do not know as yet what long-term effect this will have on Ben, but we will monitor his condition. To conclude, Ben has been very helpful since, and I feel he poses no threat to this country. If anything, he could be a great asset." Robert Jenkins-Smyth sat back down.

"Thank you, Robert" the home secretary said, remaining seated. "Is there anything anybody wants to add?" Home Secretary Adams asked.

Lizzie stood up. "Yes sir." she said out loud and clear. "Could it be possible that Ratzilla can disappear just like Ben? After all, we have launched the largest and most comprehensive manhunt this country has ever known and have found no trace of Ratzilla."

"If he disappeared like me, then there would have been a pile of clothes," Ben mumbled to himself.

"What do you think happened then young lady?" Adams asked.

Young lady, Lizzie thought to herself, *if they don't think I'm as good as them. Well, I'll show them how clever I am.*

"Maybe the people who sent him the gun and instructions got tired of his time wasting and came to get him and their gun," Lizzie remarked. "We did find a bag containing his passport and full of money not far from the warehouse, with Ratzilla's fingerprints on and his DNA on a pair of underpants. Why would he leave his getaway money, passport, and clothes behind? It doesn't make any sense."

"If they killed him, then why not leave a body behind for us to find? That would take some heat off, don't you think?" Robert said. "He could have left the money deliberately to throw us off his scent. For all we know, he might have a lot more money stashed elsewhere."

"But Sir," Lizzie continued, "there are witnesses in the area that said they saw a bright light, a very bright light, just before we found the bag, and others say they also saw this purple haze or smoke."

"He could have fired his gun at somebody, which creates a bright light," Bertrand interrupted.

"We didn't find any more bodies or stunned people, so I doubt that." Lizzie replied fiercely "And what about the purple haze?"

"That's enough!" Robert barked, "we will continue looking for him. No stone will be left unturned. As with everything about this case, there are always more questions than answers. Meanwhile, all potential targets have been put on high alert and the search continues. That will be all." Robert said.

"Just one moment, Robert, I need to discuss something with you alone." Adams told Robert Jenkins-Smyth.

Once the room had cleared, the home secretary updated Robert on a twist of events that he thought he could not mention at the meeting.

"We think, no," he said, "we are positive another gun has turned up in America. New York City to be exact. The Americans are denying it, but we have our sources, and the gun is the same as the one Ratzilla has."

"Can't we pool our information, Sir?" Robert asked. "After all, we are close allies."

"Yes, we are allies," Adams replied, "but the Americans see the potential of this weapon, and they won't share it with anyone, not even us. Also, the Prime minister says they have been making enquiries about Ben at the very highest levels, so they probably know about our gun too. They have their sources just as we have ours. We don't think they know Ben's identity yet but it's only a matter of time."

"So how did the Americans obtain the gun? And do they have the operative?" Robert enquired.

"We don't know. Once the gun was discovered, everything went silent, we have no way of finding out." Adams replied. "Or do we, Robert? I need you to find out as much as you can about what the Americans know about the gun and about anything they know about Ben and his ability to disappear."

"Thank you, sir, I will see what I can do." Robert said.

"It has to be very discreet. We don't want to upset our close allies, the Americans, do we?" Adams said. "This has to be totally unofficial. Unfortunately, the buck stops with you Robert. It can't lead to me or the Prime Minister. do I make myself clear?"

"Perfectly clear Minister. I know what I have to do." Jenkins-Smyth replied.

SIXTEEN

Ben was summoned to Robert's Jenkins-Smyth's office.
"Please sit down, Ben. Would you like something to drink?"

"No thank you, Sir" Ben replied.

"How are we treating you and your father? You will let me know if you need anything won't you Ben?"

"Yes Sir," Ben said.

"Please there is no need to call me sir. My name is Robert. We should be friends, after all, we are all on the same side.

"Thank you, Robert," Ben replied." *So, why am I not allowed to leave if we are friends?* Ben thought, smiling at the same time to disguise his real feelings.

"Why have you not tried to escape Ben," Robert asked. "It's obvious we could not hold you here if you wanted to leave."

"You still have my father, and I don't want to endanger him again." Ben replied. "I also think I can be of great value to you and my country with the new skills I have acquired."

"That is quite commendable of you Ben," Robert Jenkins-Smyth said. "I think you are finding this all quite exciting Ben. An adventure, don't you think?" Robert said.

"Yes, you could say that" Ben said, "but I also want to help and maybe get back my old life and body if that's possible. The only way to find out is to help you catch Ratzilla and get that gun."

"What if I told you that another gun had been found," Robert said. "Would you be interested in helping us learn about that gun?"

"Where is this other gun and who has it?" Ben asked. "You're the British government, you should be able to get it without my help." Ben was starting to wonder where this gun could be that the British secret service was asking his help; The help of a seventeen-year-old boy.

"The gun is at Area 51, in the United States of America," Robert said. "Have you ever heard of Area 51 Ben?"

"Yes, I have heard of Area 51. It's a top-secret air force base, Edwards Air force base, about 80 miles north of Las Vegas." Ben said. "That's where the Americans do all their testing of UFO's and anything to do with things from outer space. I've read all about Roswell too, and the crashed spaceship that was taken to Area 51 and is still there to this day. Everything about Area 51 is top, top secret and the CIA have only recently acknowledged its existence. So yes, I know quite a lot about Area 51 and its connection to aliens."

"Calm down, Ben; let me explain why we need your help." Robert said. "The Americans have got hold of another gun, but they won't share the details with us because they want the gun technology for themselves. To be fair we would have done exactly the same. As for Aliens, let's not let our imagination run wild. Area 51 is a top-secret base where they carry out scientific and military research, so it would be quite normal for the Americans to take it there."

"So, what do you think I can do against the might of America?" Ben said.

"You can become invisible, Ben, find out as much as you can about the gun and report back to us," Robert said. "You don't have to steal it. That would be crazy."

"You want me to spy against the Americans," Ben said.

"You would be doing it for your country." Robert replied.

"Once we have the technology, we could help those three loyal and dedicated operatives to recover and join their poor suffering families. Maybe even reverse what has happened to you," Robert said. "We will provide you with all the backup and support you will need."

"Can I choose my support team?" Ben asked.

"This is a very serious situation," Robert stated. "Only trained personnel could be involved. Who do you have in mind?"

"I want Lizzie to accompany me if I go to America." Ben demanded.

"But Lizzie isn't a field operative; she's not trained for field work." Robert said. "I'm sorry but I can't sanction that, this is going to be a very difficult operation and we have field operatives who would be of great help to you. If this is more than just work, I can arrange for you to see each other on your return. It's obvious you like her Ben, she's a very pretty girl."

"No, it's not that," although deep down it really was. "Lizzie is very bright and will be a big help. Also, I can trust her; if you want me to go then she must come with me." Ben demanded again.

Robert looked at Ben for a couple of seconds then made a call to his secretary. "Please ask Lizzie Summer to come up to my office immediately, it's urgent. You may be right Ben. Nobody would suspect two young kids on holiday."

Ben sat there in his chair thinking to himself. *What have I just got myself and Lizzie into? She will never forgive me let alone go out on a date with me now.*

Ben had become very good at controlling his heart rate; he'd had a lot of spare time recently to practice. If only his father could come up with a way to keep his clothes on. It would save a lot of embarrassing moments. He could still recall the expression on his father's face when Ben disappeared in front of him for the first time. Ben knew that being a scientist, his father thought everything had a logical explanation and that matter did not just disappear and reappear again. The fact that Ben could control this all by making his heart rate rise and fall made it even more unbelievable.

"This is all way beyond the science we know about today. It could be the future." Professor Norton kept saying. "Has someone travelled back in time?" Ben heard his father say more than once.

There was a knock on the door and Lizzie entered Robert's office. "You asked to see me, sir?" Lizzie asked.

"Yes, Miss Summer. Please, sit down," Robert replied. "I have a request, and only a request mind you, regarding a very important mission that requires certain skills which you possess. I have asked Ben here to travel to America to gather some information and he has requested that you accompany him. This mission has not been sanctioned by Her Majesties Government. It's unofficial so you will be on your own, so to speak. Do I make myself clear young lady?"

Young Lady, thought Lizzie, *if anyone calls me that again I will punch them even if it is the home secretary or the head of MI6.* "Yes, I accept." came the reply from Lizzie without hesitation. Lizzie then thought about her overzealous reply without waiting to hear what she had just volunteered for.

"Good, that's splendid," Robert said. "Ben, go and get some rest while I brief Miss Summer with the details. You'll be leaving tonight from Heathrow airport bound for Las Vegas where you will pick up a hire car for your touring holiday with your girlfriend."

"Will that be first class?" remarked Ben cheekily.

"No." came Roberts reply, "you are not to attract attention to yourselves at all. Just two young kids going to America on holiday. Normal economy class it has to be I'm afraid."

Ben got up and left the room, not before turning to glance at Lizzie. Was she pleased with him or not? He thought not, in fact she looked quite angry. As he walked out, he couldn't help thinking: *What have I done? She hates me now. MI6 speak to you as if they own you, well they don't* he thought to himself. *I'm my own man, I'll be eighteen soon. Also, I've got them to let me spend some time with Lizzie. I'll have to work my charms on her. Who am I kidding,* thought Ben, *I have no charms with women? Where is my passport?* Ben wondered.

Meanwhile, back in Robert Jenkins-Smyth's office, Lizzie was listening quite intently to her instructions. She is finally going out into the field on a very important mission. Lizzie struggled but managed to subdue her emotions, she was so excited, but she wasn't going to jeopardise this opportunity, she would be totally calm and professional.

"We have reason to believe that the gun has been moved to Area 51 in Nevada," Robert continued.

"You will escort Ben to the outer perimeter of the base and equip him as necessary, but you are under no circumstances to get caught with him by the Americans, because it will cause a very big diplomatic problem for all of us back here. You are to leave him there if he is caught and return home. Do I make myself perfectly clear young lady?" Robert continued. "Her Majesties Government will take the stance that you are trying to help your young boyfriend recover the gun so he can try and turn his life back. As you have no field experience, the Americans will assume that this is correct. We would not send a total novice on such an important mission."

"Yes Sir," Lizzie replied, trying very hard not to show her anger at being called young lady again.

Lizzie left the office and made her way home. *They think I can't do this; I'll show them. After all*, Lizzie thought, *how difficult could it be to break into the most secure base in the USA using a seventeen-year-old boy that can disappear, walk through walls and fly?* She gave a nervous laugh whilst holding back her real fear and trepidation. *We will do this. I'll make Ben into a real super spy.*

As soon as Lizzie left Robert's office, he put a call out to his secretary.

"Get me Briggs, now." he demanded.

John Briggs had worked for MI6 since he left the army. A heavily decorated member of the SAS, he was still working for his country, which he would die for, but not without one hell of a fight. John Briggs would do things a little unorthodox if required. He was an enforcer when needed. Robert Jenkins-Smyth was his old commanding officer and had recruited him personally.

Briggs entered Jenkins-Smyth's office and stood to attention.

"You sent for me, sir" Briggs said.

"Yes, I did John," Jenkins-Smyth replied. "I have a babysitting job for you of the utmost secrecy. I am sending two novices to America to recover information about a new weapon the Americans have got hold of but won't share with us. The first is a young operative by the name of Lizzie Summer who works in our surveillance department, and a young man by the name of Ben Norton. Um…" Robert Jenkins-Smyth hesitated. "How do I put this. Ben Norton possesses the skill to make himself vanish."

Jenkins-Smyth paused to see how Briggs would react.

"Vanish did you say, Sir?" Briggs enquired.

"Yes. Vanish," Jenkins-Smyth replied. "This weapon if it is what we think, gave the boy his powers and we want it. But it is being held in Area 51 and as you know, not the easiest of places to break into and steal something of that importance. Your mission is to follow the boy and the young lady to America with a small team and look after them. Once the weapon is located, you will use the boy to remove the weapon from Area 51 and return with the boy and weapon to the UK. It goes without mention that you are on your own as MI6 can't be connected to this operation. The girl is expendable, but the boy is far too valuable to lose, or worse still, let the Americans get hold of. I have no choice but to risk the boy as time is of the essence. I can't express to you how important the boy is to us, Briggs. Don't let any harm befall him or worse still let the Americans get hold of him."

"I understand Sir," Briggs said as he took a brown file from Jenkins-Smyth and left the office, but not before he turned and asked "You did say vanish, Sir?"

Ben was fuming. He had heard the whole conversation. Ben floated back invisibly to Jenkins-Smyth's office because he thought they had agreed to his demand over Lizzie too easily, and wanted to hear what she really thought of Ben. Ben always knew they were just using him but the way they dismissed Lizzie's life was inexcusable. *I will get the weapon back but for myself. And I will protect Lizzie. I will tell father it's a holiday treat for services to my country. I must try and catch him when he is busy, he'll just look up and say enjoy yourself, be good, and don't' drink any alcohol, just like all Dads do when their sons go abroad.*

SEVENTEEN

Ratzilla could hear the gunfire as he was making his way through the sewers as quietly as he could, but at the same time trying to travel as fast as he could. Then a deafening silence; either his foolish four had won or more likely they had been captured or killed. He was holding the gun in his right hand as tight as he could, knowing that if he was confronted he would have to fight his way out or he would be killed.

It seemed to Ratzilla that the sewer went on for miles but it was only a few hundred meters before he came to the hidden exit he had accidently discovered years earlier which led him to use the derelict warehouse as his base.

He slowly made his way up to the street above being very careful not to be heard or seen by anyone. Once he was sure, he started to make his way as fast as he could without actually running. Suddenly he was lit up with the brightest light he had ever encountered; it was coming from above his head.MI6 must have found him already, but he could not hear any rotary blades from a helicopter. *What the hell is going on.* He froze trying to decide whether to run or give up, just like a scared animal staring into a car's headlights.

Before Ratzilla could even make that decision, he was enveloped with an odourless purple smoke.

Once the smoke had disappeared, Ratzilla had gone too.

No light, no Ratzilla and no gun. Just a bag full of money, a passport, and a spare pair of underpants.

EIGHTEEN

After going through customs and security more smoothly than normal, Ben and Lizzie got themselves ready for the long flight to America. Ben had not had the chance to tell Lizzie what he had overheard in Jenkins-Smyth's office because they had been taken to the airport and checked in for their flight by MI6 personnel. Even telling her on the flight would be difficult, travelling in economy. All the seats were so close together and Ben could not take the chance that they wouldn't be overheard. Ben had also not been able to spot John Briggs at the airport, where he was hoping to see who Briggs' accomplices were. There was one thing thought Ben that gave them the advantage: it was that he knew what MI6 was up to, but MI6 didn't know that Ben knew about John Briggs. Still, Briggs was going to be their insurance just in case things didn't go to plan.

After being airborne for a couple of hours, Ben got up to go to the toilet. He decided to go to the front cubicle, slowly scanning all the passengers on his left and right to see if anyone was paying him more attention than they should have. There were the usual suited businessmen working away on their laptops, tablets and papers, ready for their business meeting; a couple of nun's reading (probably Bibles, Ben thought); a young family with two very small children, (it was going to be a long flight for those parents.) On reaching the toilet cubicle it became apparent to him that the security people were selected for their ability to blend in, and they would never give themselves away. Real life is not like the films he thought to himself. John Briggs was probably on another flight anyway because Lizzie might have seen him before at MI6 headquarters and Lizzie never forgot a face ever. A couple of hours later Ben went to the rear toilet and again he could not see anyone acting suspiciously so he decided to accept they were around and would only identify themselves if Ben and Lizzie got into any trouble. On returning to his seat, Lizzie asked him why he was acting a bit strange, always checking on anyone who walked past their seats. Ben slowly checked the passengers all around him and they all had headphones on and were watching the film in front. Ben started to whisper in Lizzie's ear telling her about his return to Jenkins-Smyth's office and all about John Briggs.

"I have come across that name before on another case that was headed by Jenkins-Smyth," Lizzie said. "Briggs caught and arrested three terrorists that had been on the wanted list for years. It would have been very impressive but there were no files regarding the case and nobody dare ask for details. Briggs always seems to work in the shadows, very dangerous by all accounts but also very effective."

"It's good he's on our side then." Ben remarked.

"So, I'm expendable then? Well, that doesn't surprise me," Lizzie said. "But you Ben are so precious, how does that make you feel?", trying really hard not to laugh.

"Like a freak" Ben replied.

"Your country comes first in this game," Lizzie said, without even a hint of resentment. "You have a unique talent now, Ben, so be proud you are helping your country in these dark times."

"I still feel like a freak though," Ben repeated.

"Have a rest, Ben," Lizzie said, "just relax, the flight will be over soon. A freak you are definitely not."

Once the plane had landed they made their way through security without any problems, picked up their luggage and were looking for signs to collect their hire car.

"It's down here," Lizzie instructed Ben, as they followed the signs for the hire car companies.

Lizzie noticed up ahead a number of what appeared to her as secret service personnel; they all had the dark suits, dark glasses, and the regulation earpieces, and were herding someone along. She couldn't make out at first who it was that was surrounded by dark suits, then her super memory skills kicked in and she recognised who it was. Someone very important it definitely is, she realised.

"It's the President's daughter Ruby Carlsen," she whispered to Ben.

Then there was an enormous bang. It was the loudest thing Ben had ever heard. Glass was shattering everywhere and flying through the air, smoke filled the air and people were screaming and running all around them. Ben turned to check on Lizzie. She was covered in broken glass but not bleeding. He was so relieved.

"Are you Ok?" he asked.

"Yes, I'm fine just a bit shaken; my ears are still ringing though." Lizzie shouted.

"Look after my clothes and bag; I will meet you at the hotel in Vegas" Ben said.

"Where are you going Ben? Keep a low profile we were told!" Lizzie said. But it was too late. There was a pile of Ben's clothes and mobile phone on the floor, and he had vanished.

Ben drifted up and out of the building to escape the smoke and see where the secret service agents were. They, or more to the point their client, was obviously the target of this attack. Ben saw this young girl, Ruby Carlsen, being pushed into a black van which sped off, but not by the secret service. *I have to follow them* Ben thought. He climbed as high as he could and followed the van as it drove out of the airport which was now covered with blue flashing lights. After about 20 minutes they came to a disused factory and dragged the now blindfolded girl out of the van and took her inside. The van drove off. *I need to go down and see how many there are,* Ben thought, *and get in touch with Lizzie who can call the police.* Ben made a thorough reccy of the old factory, then left to try and contact Lizzie. *I can't go to our hotel,* Ben thought, *as it was too far and they may move the girl somewhere else. I'm going to have to call her, but how, I don't have my phone, any money or any clothes.*

Ben decided to re-enter the factory and see if he could steal one of the mobile phones from the kidnappers. Once back inside, he looked for any opportunity to speak to the girl and assure her she would be rescued soon. There were 7 kidnappers all huddled around the poor frightened girl who was now tied to a chair. They were speaking in a foreign language which Ben could not understand. Eventually, one of the gang left the others and walked to the far end of the factory, and went through a door. *I'll follow him,* Ben thought, *if he's away from the others I may get a chance to do something.* Ben followed the man who made his way up a back staircase to the toilets, went into one of the cubicles and locked the door. Whilst following the man, Ben had noticed an old pair of overalls hanging up in an old changing room.

Ben went back for the overalls and reappeared, quickly putting them on, and whilst heading back towards the toilets, he was looking for a weapon of some sort. *I've never even had a fight before let alone knocked someone out* Ben thought to himself. *Right, stay calm Ben or you will disappear again. They can't hurt me, so let's just do it and save this girl. I'll be a hero* he thought, completely forgetting what Jenkins-Smyth had said about keeping a low profile. Ben noticed a broken chair leg. *That would do just fine* he thought. He quietly made his way back to the toilets, but as he was about to position himself just outside the man's cubicle, the door swung open and the two of them came face to face. They just stared at each other for a couple of seconds, both frozen with shock. Ben was holding his chair leg, and the man his mobile phone. Ben was so shocked, his heart uncontrollably started to pound. As Ben's overalls and chair leg fell to the floor, the man screamed, dropped his phone, and ran out of the toilets as if he had seen a ghost. Well, he had sort of.

Ben could hear the man's screams faintly disappear in the distance. *That was close* Ben thought. He reappeared, dressed himself again, then picked up the phone and chair leg and quickly left the toilets.

A couple of minutes later, the man returned with a couple of his friends. He was gesticulating and pointing to the very spot he saw Ben, but the clothes and chair leg were gone. But more importantly, his phone was gone too. They hurried back to the others and had a conflab about what to do next. Meanwhile, Ben was praising his luck because the phone was unlocked, and he could call the police for help immediately.

Ben remembered from his love of films that in America the number you called for police was 911. Ben rang the number, then tried to explain what had happened and where he was now. He told the operator that he was a tourist arriving that day from London at the airport and saw the kidnapping, and managed to climb onto the van without the gang noticing, leading him to where they were holding the President's daughter. But he didn't know where he was, "an old factory" he said.

"Just one moment, Sir. Did you say you witnessed the kidnapping of President Carlsen's daughter Ruby and you are there now?" The police operator said.

"Yes, that's correct" Ben said. "But they may have spotted me and maybe getting ready to leave. You must send help immediately. All I noticed is that it's an old cement factory that is now all boarded up."

"You say it's an old factory and it took you about 20 minutes from the airport to get there, is that correct sir?"

"Yes, that's correct," Ben replied, "please get here quickly.

"Don't you worry none; the police operator said I know where that is. Help will be with you as soon as possible. May I just say you speak really nice sir, are you Australian?"

"No, I'm British," Ben replied. "I will try to keep an eye on what's going on but I am alone and there are 7 of them. They are heavily armed," Ben told the operator, "and speaking in a foreign accent."

"We have your location, Sir, and are sending help immediately" the operator said. "Is it safe for you to go inside and see what they are doing?"

"Yes, that will be fine, I will leave the phone on so you can hear what is going on but please don't speak as they may hear it." Ben said.

Ben made his way back inside the central section of the factory and managed to place the phone about 20 metres from where they were holding Ruby. There was a real panic now, the kidnappers were calling people and shouting down their phones and at each other, running around, gathering all their weapons as if they were going to leave in a hurry. Ben decided that he must delay them somehow and protect the girl until the police arrive. *But how? They think this place is haunted, I'll give them the run-around, that should give the police some time.* Ben left the phone out of sight and made his way behind the kidnappers. He then started to make what he thought were ghost noises, howling and wooing. Then there was silence. *It was working* Ben thought. The next thing Ben heard was the clicking of a gun trigger being made ready to fire right next to his ear. Ben took a big gulp then slowly turned to face the man with the gun aimed at Ben's head. At first the man shouted something he did not understand then shoved him to walk towards where the girl was being held. Not one of my best ideas, Ben thought to himself, as he was being led out towards the gang.

"Who are you?" a man asked in a thick accent.

Ben had decided that he could delay them leaving by not disappearing. "I live here," Ben replied. "I am homeless."

"You speak very funny; you are not American?" The man asked.

"No, I'm English, I came here on holiday but had all my stuff stolen." Ben replied.

The man said something in his own language to the others; they then pushed Ben into a chair next to Ruby and tied him up too.

Ben turned to Ruby and smiled. He mouthed out to her "the cavalry is on its way." Ruby looked back and gave him a very puzzled look; she couldn't lip read. Ben just smiled then quickly said it will all be ok very soon.

"No talking!" said the man.

Not long after, that there were a series of loud bangs and then the air was filed with smoke. A number of shots rang out. Before Ben could even try to work out what was going on or even if he had been shot, he was surrounded by very heavily armed soldiers with masks and night vision goggles. They grabbed Ruby and took her out first, then they picked Ben up, eyes stinging from the smoke and choking for air, still tied to the chair, and carried him out too. The fresh air outside was a relief to Ben. All he kept saying to himself was keep calm Ben, just keep very calm. It would look very bad for him if he disappeared in front if all these soldiers. It then dawned on him; he had saved the President's daughter from these terrorists. He was a hero after all. If only they knew how he did it, they would be calling him a superhero. At this moment it dawned on Ben what he had done, and could hear Robert Jenkins-Smyth's voice ringing in his ears. Keep a low profile was the only instruction he had been given and he broke it within the first hour of them landing in America.

*

"Get me Briggs!" shouted Robert Jenkins-Smyth down his telephone.

"Yes, Sir" came the polite reply from his secretary. She knew when her boss was in this sort of mood, you just did what he wanted without any fuss and kept your head down. "I have John Briggs for you Sir on a secure line."

"How the hell did you allow this to happen?" demanded Jenkins-Smyth. "Your brief was to babysit two wet behind the ears kids," he continued, before Briggs could reply.

"I think the boy suspected something was not quite right sir, even on the plane he kept marching up and down looking for someone or something. But my people are too good to get spotted. Then he and the girl started whispering so we made sure we kept a very close eye on them when they landed."

"How the devil then did he get away from you and rescue Ruby Carlsen?" Jenkins-Smyth demanded. "The damn president's daughter no less. Keep a low profile was his and your brief. well, you managed that really well didn't you Briggs. Don't tell me he disappeared in broad daylight in the middle of an airport with wall-to-wall CCTV…"

"Well yes, sort of" Briggs replied. "The kidnappers set off stun grenades and a small bomb to grab hold of Ruby Carlsen from her secret service detail. Before my team could get to Ben and Lizzie, he just vanished, left a pile of clothes on the floor and was gone. Even though my team had been briefed about Ben, it was still a shock for them the first time it happened in front of them. I then gave an order to back off and leave the girl just in case Ben came back straight away. There was lots of smoke and panic so there is a good chance nobody spotted him vanish. As a precaution,

I have made arrangements to replace the relevant CCTV footage with corrupt files."

"You better be right, Briggs, or this whole mission is not only finished, but we may have lost Ben as well." Jenkins-Smyth said. "You just keep an eye on Lizzie Summer while I contact the Americans regarding Ben. And Briggs, we can't afford any more errors, do you understand?"

"Yes, Sir" Briggs replied.

Now to find out what the Americans know about Ben, thought Jenkins-Smyth, *without raising suspicion. Damn fool Ben, if only you knew how valuable you are.*

NINETEEN

Ben was taken to a non-descript office somewhere in Las Vegas; that much he knew but not a lot else. He was led by five heavily armed officers into an interrogation suite. *Not again,* thought Ben, when he realised what was happening. *I should have done what Lizzie said and just stayed out of it. But I didn't and now I'm a hero. They can't treat me like this.* he decided.

"Am I under arrest?" demanded Ben when they sat him down behind a small desk.

"No Sir you are not under arrest." came the reply from a tall blonde man, about forty.

"My name is Agent Brad Stringer and I'm leading this enquiry. We need your help to piece together what happened today at the airport and subsequently at the factory. The United States Government and its people are very grateful to you for your bravery and help in the rescuing of Ruby Carlsen, the President's daughter."

Ben had had enough time to come up with a believable enough story without telling them about his ability to vanish.

"I'm here on holiday with my girlfriend Lizzie," Ben started. "We were walking towards the car hire area in the airport when there was an explosion; I panicked and just ran to get out. I'm so ashamed. I forgot all about my girlfriend Lizzie, I panicked. Once outside I noticed these men grabbing this girl, who was kicking and screaming, and throwing her into this van. Without thinking, I ran and grabbed onto the van and jumped on the back just as it was driving away."

"So, let's see if this is correct. There is an explosion, you panic and leave your girlfriend inside the airport, but once outside you are calm enough to attempt to rescue this unknown girl by jumping onto the back of their getaway vehicle?" Brad enquired.

"I know who she is," Ben replied. "I've seen her on TV and I quite like her, I think she's cute." Ben was struggling to make his story more believable.

"You're telling us you have a crush on the President's daughter?" Brad stated.

"Not quite a crush, I think she's pretty and ok." Ben replied.

"So, you knew she was a very important person and you jumped onto the vehicle?" Brad continued. "Then what happened?"

"It was very hard but I managed to hang onto the back of the van," Ben said. "The journey thankfully was not too long. When they arrived at the factory, they slowed down enough for me to jump off. I waited then went inside to see what was going on."

"Why did you not just go for help or call the cops?" Brad asked.

"I didn't know where I was so by calling the police at this point would not have helped and I wanted to make sure Ruby was ok." Ben replied.

"What happened to your clothes? Or did you fly to the U.S in these dirty overalls you are wearing now." Brad asked.

This threw Ben. He had not thought about the clothes. This made him hesitate for a couple of seconds.

"When I jumped off the van I fell into a muddy puddle and they got filthy dirty and soaking wet, so when I was inside, I found these," Ben said pointing down to his overalls. I could not stay in wet clothes; I might have caught a cold. After all I am on holiday."

"So where are your clothes Ben?" Brad asked again.

"I dumped them in the factory, I didn't want the kidnappers to find my clothes or me," Ben said, raising his voice, putting him on the defensive. "Why are you asking me all these questions? Do you think I was involved in all this?"

"No, not at all but we need to get all the facts straight. It's our job; we think you did great kid," Brad remarked.

The door swung open and a man in a uniform burst in, a very senior officer's type of uniform with row upon row of medals. He summoned Brad over to him and spoke very quietly.

Brad came back over to Ben and warmly shook his hand.

"You have been invited to the White House in Washington DC where the President and Ruby would like to thank you in person. General Mark's men will escort you to your hotel in Las Vegas where you and your girlfriend will pack your things and then will be taken by Airforce One to Washington DC tonight."

Ben stood up and followed the General out of the room, saying to himself, *of course the White house is in Washington DC, who doesn't know that?*

"There is something not right about this kid," Brad turned and said to one of his colleagues after Ben had left the room. "His story makes no sense at all; firstly, he leaves his girlfriend at the airport and climbs onto the kidnapper's getaway vehicle. But we can't find one person who sees this kid hanging onto the back of the vehicle in broad daylight. Then there is this story about the clothes. Why dump your clothes, and where is this puddle in the Nevada desert? It's so hot here the clothes would dry in seconds if they got wet. I want you to go back to the factory and look for this "puddle" and find his clothes. Check the security tapes at the airport to see what he was wearing. I'm going to join them in Washington."

TWENTY

John Briggs was viewing the CCTV footage of the airport when the explosion took place. He could easily pick out Ben and Lizzie, even with all the smoke and confusion of people running around in a panic. Then he saw it for himself. Ben just vanishes into thin air. All you see is his clothes just fall to the ground in a heap and Lizzie quickly picking them up and putting them in her bag.

"Good work Cooper," as Briggs turned to his second in command. "Really good work, no one saw you I hope?"

"No, Sir, we were very careful, especially with the heightened security after the bombing." Stephanie Cooper replied. "Even in these days of terrorist attacks nobody suspects a couple of nuns, and it's amazing how much you can hide under your habit" she said.

"Did you have time to replace the CCTV with spoilt files?" Briggs asked.

"Yes sir," Cooper replied. "A good clean job, even if I say so myself."

"Our hero and his girlfriend have been summoned to the White House to be thanked by the president personally,"

Briggs stated. "We'll be following them; the mission is still on according to London. Though with all this publicity they haven't got a prayer of getting anywhere near Area 51."

Agent Brad Stringer was crimson with rage.

"What do you mean, all the CCTV files are useless!?" he shouted at his men. "It's an international airport what sort of equipment are we using there, hundred year old brownie cameras?"

"No, Sir," came the reply from a visibly shaking young man. "The equipment is state of the art modern recording equipment but the files are all corrupt, nothing has been saved."

"Don't we have a backup system for this scenario?" Brad Stringer demanded.

"No, Sir," came the reply from another agent. "This has never happened before. We have sent the files to our lab to have them tested, just in case they have been tampered with by the kidnappers or their accomplices."

"This whole case is starting to smell worse and worse by the minute," Brad said to himself. "How confident are these people that they can come back to a major crime scene and tamper with our security systems then just walk out and nobody sees or hears anything? This is the United States of America! We lead the world in security," now shouting out loud making his whole team back away. *Or do we?* he thought. *This seems like it has the backing of a major player or country.*

"I'm on my way to Washington if you need me, call me on my cell phone as soon as you find the kids clothes." *I'm going to get to the bottom of this* he thought; *even the president could be in danger.*

"This certainly beats flying economy" Ben said to Lizzie, who was sitting opposite him. They were both sitting in very large luxurious leather seats sipping non-alcoholic cocktails.

"So, this is what Air Force One is like inside," Lizzie remarked, calmly surveying everything and everyone, thinking *this is what I would be trained to do if I was out in the field.* "You sure know how to travel in class, General. Was this plane laid on just for us?" Lizzie asked the General.

"No, Miss Summer, it was intended to take Ruby Carlsen back to Washington DC this evening for a very special engagement," replied General Mark. "There are actually two of these and Air Force One is the plane that carries the President."

"Thank you very much," said Lizzie, "your generosity is overwhelming."

"That's very kind of you" replied General Mark, sitting adjacent to the two VIP's. "Please enjoy our hospitality, our ETA is 1800 hours." Noticing Ben's blank look, he continued. "We will be touching down in Washington D.C in a couple of hours at 6 pm. Are you two hungry? Can I get the chef to make you something to eat?" General Mark pressed a button by his seat and within a few seconds a waiter came over.

"Yes, Sir, how may I be of assistance to you General?" the waiter asked.

"Please make our guests something to eat, whatever they want" replied the General.

Ben sat bolt upright when he heard the words "whatever you want".

"Can I have a fry up please?" asked Ben after a minute's hesitation. "I'm still on London time and my stomach needs something stodgy."

Lizzie glanced at Ben the way a wife would stare at her husband when he says something inappropriate in proper company.

"I'm so sorry, Sir, we have most things, but I've never served stodgy before." The waited meekly replied.

"Sausages, bacon that's what we call stodgy back in England." Ben explained.

"Oh, I see Sir, you would like a cooked breakfast." The waiter said. "And how would you like your eggs sir, easy over, sunny side up, poached, scrambled, boiled soft, boiled hard, eggs Benedict?"

"Eggs Benedict, I like that, you're quite funny. Just plain fried and runny please," Ben interrupted.

"May I just have some fruit?" Lizzie asked.

"Yes Madam," came the reply from the waiter.

"Did you bring anything formal to wear with you to the states?" The general enquired, "because tomorrow night there is going to be a state dinner held in your honour, and its black tie."

"No, nothing," Lizzie and Ben replied in unison.

"Right then." said the General. "We will take you to your hotel when we arrive tonight, where you can rest, and I will send a car for you tomorrow morning to take you shopping."

"Hotel?" enquired Lizzie, "what sort of hotel? And shopping for evening wear, we don't have a lot of money left."

You'll be staying at the Jefferson, a fine 5 star hotel just four blocks from the White House," stated the General, "compliments of the United States Government. You can order any food you like and charge it to your room, but no alcohol as you are both under 21. As for your clothes, we will buy you whatever you need. It's a very small price to pay for saving the life of the President's daughter. You are a hero, young man, and you will be shown real American hospitality."

Lizzie just smiled at the General, whilst inside she was repeating to herself *you are a hero, young man. So much for keeping a low profile* she thought. *I will have to contact London somehow and get fresh instructions. My first and probably my last mission thanks to Ben, though I shouldn't be too hard on him because I knew he was doing the right thing at the time. He has also told me what Jenkins-Smyth really thinks of me, and that's not a lot. Ben thinks he can still pull this off so I'm going to back him up as much as I can. If this is going to be my last mission, I'm going to make sure it's one to remember.*

The time flew by and soon they had landed and taxied to a quiet part of the airport. No security checks for them, just a short walk to a waiting limo. That's when Ben had his idea for getting into Area 51. Ben just smiled at Lizzie and said, "I think we can still get Uncle Robert his present you know."

"What is it that your Uncle Robert wants from America?" the General asked. "I'm sure I can arrange to get it for you."

"No thank you" General Lizzie quickly replied, "it's not that important", at the same time giving Ben a very quizzical look and wishing it was that simple that you could get an American General to just get the Gun for you straight out of Area 51. If only.

It was a short drive to the hotel; having motorcycle outriders escorting them meant they cruised through the early evening traffic like a hot knife through butter. They soon pulled into a small crescent drive and stopped outside this grand stone building with a large ornate metal cover over the front door. A very smart uniformed man quickly came to the car doors and opened them with a "Welcome to the Jefferson Hotel". The entourage led by General Mark quickly made its way through the grand entrance and into the reception area with its black and white marble floor and beautiful décor. No checking in for them like normal people, this had all been taken care of in advance. Ben and Lizzie were really enjoying being treated like VIP's. They were taken up to their hotel suite where a guard was already posted outside.

"We don't think you are in any immediate danger", the General tried to assure them, "but we can't and won't take any chances, these are very difficult times."

Not in danger Lizzie thought, *but they* were *being followed.* Those two ladies sitting in the reception lounge of the hotel were the same two dressed as nuns on the plane from England, of that Lizzie was totally sure. Were they British keeping an eye on them or were they the terrorists? *We will probably soon find out* she thought.

"Oh wow!" Ben said out loud when he saw inside the hotel suite. Then noticing the very large double bed in the adjacent bedroom he started to blush. "Calm down" he said to himself "I can't disappear in front of the American secret service" as he turned to look at Lizzie who had also seen the large bed.

"This is wonderful" Lizzie said to the General, "thank you very much. Are we allowed to go out and see the sights tonight on our own, or will we have a chaperone?" she enquired.

"I'm sorry but for tonight you are under the care of the United States Government, and we would like you to have an escort wherever you go outside this hotel suite." The General stated very matter of fact like. "But after tomorrow night's event you will be free to go anywhere you like and continue your vacation. Air Force One is on standby to take you anywhere you wish."

Ben and Lizzie just stood in the middle of their bedroom staring at each other, but they had very different thoughts running through their minds. Lizzie was thinking about how to get in touch with London, being aware that the room was probably bugged. Ben was wondering if they would be sleeping in that bed together or should he offer to sleep on the couch in the living room. Ben quickly accepted he was going to sleep on the couch.

After everyone had left, they were given the instructions that if they needed anything they should just ring reception. If they wanted to go out, they needed to let agent Walker know. He was their guard stationed outside and he would make the necessary arrangements. Ben went to speak but before a single word came out Lizzie put her index finger to his lips to stop him saying anything. She then left the bedroom and returned to the living room closely followed by a bemused Ben. Lizzie made her way to the desk in the far corner of this vast and beautifully decorated room, she picked up the pad and pen both bearing the crest of the hotel and started to write frantically. *This room is probably bugged*, the first note said. *We must carry on as if we are a couple and on holiday*, the second note continued. *Just be very careful what you say*, was on the third note.

We are being followed but I don't know if they are British or not, Lizzie wrote on the fourth note.

Ben just stared in amazement at this calm, efficient and very clever lady. How did she work all that out and who was it that was following them? Hopefully, it was John Briggs and his team.

After tomorrow night we can resume our mission without all these security people watching our every move. Ben just nodded his acceptance after every note and then took the pad from her.

Do you want me to do my thing and get a message to London?

Lizzie just shook her head. Taking the note pad back she wrote, *we may be under visual surveillance as well so we must give them nothing to suspect us of. We will even have to sleep in the bed together; I hope you are Ok with that Ben*, the last note read. She then smiled at Ben. *We must stop this note writing as well because it must also look very suspicious.*

Is she teasing me or does she fancy me? Ben thought. *No, Lizzie is on a mission for her country and nothing will stop her from doing her best.* That's when Ben decided that to win her over he would have to have that approach as well and prove to her he was not just a naïve young boy, but could be relied upon to complete his, no, their mission. Ben just smiled back; *they are both on the same page now,* he thought.

"What would you like to do tonight babe?" Ben said loud enough for even agent Walker to hear without any listening devices. "Shall we hit a night club?"

Lizzie smiled at Ben and his overacting. *He was funny,* she thought, *I think we could be good friends when this is over.* "What about going to the theatre?" Lizzie said out loud, "do you think we can get tickets for any show we want?" She then glanced down at her watch and realised the time. "It's too late for the Theatre" she remarked, "let's check the paper and see what's on locally."

"'The Greatest'" shouted Ben, "let's go and see 'The Greatest'. I saw an advertisement as we came through the city, they are in concert here tonight, the best band ever! I tried to get tickets for them back in London but they sold out after a few minutes. Let's see if the United States hospitality can come up with 'The Greatest' tickets."

"Agent Walker, would it be possible to get tickets for a concert tonight?" Ben asked popping his body round the hotel door. "It's probably sold out though."

"Who do you want to see?" asked agent Walker.

"'The Greatest'" Ben replied.

"You're in luck sir, I was taken off a duty tonight at their concert, I'm sure we can sort something out. Just let me make a call, I will let you know shortly."

Less than five minutes had passed when agent Walker entered the hotel suite. He had a smile that went from one side of his face to the other.

"All taken care of but we must leave in ten minutes" he said. "May I just say thank you to you both as I had been looking forward to going to 'The Greatest' concert but was pulled off that detail to take up this job here just this afternoon. I'm a huge fan, I have all their music."

"Are you our escort then?" asked Lizzie.

"I am" agent Walker replied. "I myself and several others, you are going to the concert with the First Lady and Ruby. Big fans too by all accounts, I have even heard the President sing along to their songs in the car."

"We can't keep calling you Agent Walker" Ben said. "What is your first name?"

"Agent Walker is fine sir; it's our protocol not to get too familiar just in case we have to kill you."

Ben's smile quickly disappeared from his face.

"Only kidding sir, my sense of humour is going to get me into a lot of trouble one of these days but I can't help it. Agent Walker stated. Don't worry though I'm better at keeping you safe than telling jokes."

"Is there a dress code for tonight?" Lizzie asked Walker, "especially if the first lady is in attendance."

"Not to my knowledge" Walker replied. All I've been told is the Limo will be here in eight minutes" he said, after checking his watch again.

"We'll be ready" Lizzie said, rushing back into the hotel room to get ready.

As the party was walking through the hotel lobby, Lizzie stumbled and fell near a couple of young women having a drink. Fortunately, a chair broke her fall. She stood up and apologised to the women just as agent Walker came over to investigate.

"Are you Ok madam?" Agent Walker enquired, as he rushed over to Lizzie's aid.

"I'm fine" Lizzie replied, "I just stumbled, must be these heels", pointing down to her shoes.

After the group left the hotel, the two ladies in the lobby got up and went to their hotel suite where John Briggs was waiting.

"Miss Summer managed to pass us a note Sir," Stephanie Cooper said, as she passed the little piece of paper over to her superior. "I don't know how she knew who we were though."

John Briggs read the note which only said, *Have you lost your Habits or has Robert got them?* John realised she was telling them she knew who they were and had spotted them on the plane.

Lizzie and Ben were taken by limo straight to the Capital One Arena where The Greatest were performing one night only as part of their world tour. Tickets were like gold dust but if you are the First Lady and daughter of the President of the United States, tickets can be found, and if you save the life of the President's daughter, you are also added to the VIP guest list. Whisked through a rear door by their very own security detail, Lizzie and Ben were taken to a sectioned off part of the arena that was surrounded by security guards. This might have been normal, or was the security increased because of what happened today at the airport?

After being offered drinks of the non-alcoholic variety, Ben and Lizzie started to enjoy the support act all alone in their very own private section of this amazing arena. Then all of a sudden, the support act stopped playing and started to applaud. Ben looked at Lizzie wondering what was going on, but Lizzie just said the real VIP's have arrived. Just then, Ruby and her mother Jade Carlsen entered the sectioned off part of the arena leaving their security detail posted at the entrance. Ruby came running over to Ben and gave him a big hug and a kiss on the cheek, saying thank you over and over again. The First Lady followed and gave Ben a very long hug, at least 20 seconds if not longer, also saying thank you repeatedly. Ben turned to Lizzie and introduced her as his friend to both Ruby and Mrs Carlsen. This made Ruby smile again. Lizzie did not know what to think.

"Benedict, please may I thank you on behalf of my husband, Ruby, and the American people. What you did today was truly heroic and we shall never be able to thank you enough for saving Ruby's life."

"I'm glad I could help," is all Ben could think of saying, as if he had only helped Ruby across the road or with some heavy shopping bags. At this point saving Ben from further embarrassment, the music started and Ruby grabbed Bens hand and dragged him over to a small makeshift dance floor and started to dance.

"I'm so sorry" Jade Carlsen turned and said to Lizzie, "My 16-year-old daughter is so excited to see Benedict again. She is not trying to steal your boyfriend."

"That's absolutely fine" replied Lizzie, "Ben and I are quite solid in our relationship", she lied.

"After all they have both been through today it's quite understandable," continued Lizzie.

"That's very mature of you, Lizzie," Jade Carlsen said.

Ben was dancing with Ruby for most of the concert and both were singing along when The Greatest came on stage. Ruby was a lovely girl, but Ben was only interested in Lizzie. Every now and then when he was dancing with Ruby, he would catch Lizzie watching as if she were a little envious of Ruby. Ben tried to dance with Lizzie but was only allowed one dance at a time before Ruby would drag him away again.

Lizzie even managed to get Agent Walker to dance with her after getting approval from both the First Lady and his superior. This made Ben very jealous but he was determined not to show it.

Ben even had a slow dance with The First Lady while the two younger ladies watched but didn't really speak to each other. Ben felt a bit awkward, so he and the First Lady only talked about food and what he liked most about American cooking.

The concert and the evening came to a halt a little too early for both Ben and Ruby, but Lizzie was looking forward to getting back to their hotel room and getting a good night's sleep, it had been a very surreal and interesting day to say the least.

Ben and Lizzie returned to the hotel suite after a great night at the concert. Agent Walker bid them goodnight and sat down outside their room.

Lizzie said to Ben "We need to get to bed as we have a long day tomorrow." She went to the TV, put it on, and selected one of the numerous music channels and turned the volume up high. Lizzie then went to the bathroom to get ready for bed.

Ben just kept saying to himself keep calm, keep calm. Ben had realised that if he got nervous he might disappear and that would ruin everything with Lizzie and the mission if they were being watched. *The TV!* he thought. "Of course! She wants to talk not dance, that's why the music is up loud. Be grown up," Ben said to himself, "be professional Ben you're on an important mission for your country.

Lizzie came out of the bathroom and slid into the large double bed wearing a white night shirt. Ben had already undressed and was in the bed waiting and fighting with himself to stay calm. Lizzie rolled over towards Ben, this made Ben very nervous, but he managed to control his pulse but only just. "Ruby really likes you Ben," Lizzie whispered to him.

"I know" Ben replied, "and guess where she has always wanted to go to since her father became President? Area 51" Ben said, before Lizzie could even answer. "She could be our ticket there and we might even get a guided tour to boot. I will work on her tomorrow night at the Presidents banquet at the White House."

"So, was that the plan you mentioned earlier? Lizzie asked. "Very clever Ben we might still pull this off yet. No, hold on Ben you didn't know Ruby wanted to go to Area 51 when you told me you had a plan, so what are you up to Ben?"

"No, my plan has changed to this," Ben said. "We can call it plan B, or should we give it a secret name? Like Alien Fortress."

"No, Plan B is fine," Lizzie said with a smile, as she rolled away from Ben. *He makes me laugh,* she thought.

Ben rolled over away from Lizzie and smiled to himself. *She thinks I'm clever, I think she is starting to fall for me. If I can pull this off, she will be so impressed.*

I will have to keep an eye on Ruby, Lizzie thought to herself. *Am I getting jealous?* she thought for a split second, and then dismissed it. *No. This is my job, which I do for my country. Feelings don't come into it*, not totally convinced.

TWENTY-ONE

Brad Stringer leaves the Oval office after failing to convince the President that Ben and Lizzie are not to be trusted and that they are working for a larger power. Brad did not know what they were after but was sure that the kidnapping was a set up so they could get closer to the President. If Ruby were the real target, she would have been dead. Brad was going to join the detail protecting Ben and Lizzie so he could keep a close eye on them.

"Why would the British try to kidnap Ruby?", President Carlsen asked Brad. "It doesn't make any sense. We know Lizzie Summer works for MI6, but she is only a researcher. Also, the British are our closest allies, so how would kidnapping Ruby benefit them? I am convinced they are not involved so stop wasting your efforts on them, we have the terrorists in custody all locked up thanks to Ben. They will soon talk and tell us everything we need to get to the bottom of the kidnapping and who was behind it."

Lizzie and Ben returned to the hotel with agent Walker carrying a dozen shopping bags which he quickly gave to the porter to take up to the suite.

On entering the lobby, Lizzie scanned the entire area for the two nuns, but she could not see them. She thought they were British but could not be sure. On entering the suite, she saw Ben rush over to the porter and retrieve his bags, he couldn't wait to try them on. As the hotel suite door closed Lizzie saw Brad Stringer talking to agent Walker. *Was he onto us?* she thought. *Why had he spent all day watching us shop when he was the lead investigator on the Ruby kidnapping? I don't like this one bit I had better warn Ben.*

Lizzie went over to the TV and selected another music channel and put the volume up high again.

Ben came out from the bedroom dressed in the best dinner suit money could buy; he looked like James Bond. *Very handsome she thought, yes very handsome indeed.*

"Can you help me with this tie?" he asked Lizzie, holding up an unmade black bow tie. "I always had cheats ties that just clip on, not these real ones. I told the General that, but he said the President was a stickler for doing things properly and he would notice if it was a cheat's tie."

Really? thought Ben, *I saved the Presidents daughters life and he would complain about a bow tie, I think it's the General that's a stickler for bow ties and for everything to be very proper.*

Lizzie had been making her father's bow tie for him for years. In fact, the first time she had to do this for her father she was so small she had to stand on a chair. Her father knew even then that if you showed Lizzie something once, she would not forget. He knew she was special even then.

As Lizzie was making Ben's tie, Ben whispered in her ear that "Uncle Robert" had been in contact, and they were to return to London straight after the Presidential banquet.

"How did they get in touch?" Lizzie asked.

"They put a note in my shopping bag" Ben replied. "I don't know how or when but it's from Briggs. You were right about the two women in reception. Briggs says well spotted, Lizzie."

"So, all of this has been a waste of time?" Lizzie whispered back.

"Not if we ignore the message and carry on as planned." Ben said.

"That's treason Ben." Lizzie replied. "We can't just ignore orders from London."

"They don't know what we know about getting into Area 51," Ben replied. "I will invite Ruby tonight to join us tomorrow. Once we are away from the secret service we can get in touch with London."

"You haven't thought this through very well Ben have you?" Lizzie said, "because I have. If we take Ruby she will have even more security after the kidnap attempt and we will be watched even closer. Also that agent Brad Stringer suspects that we are not telling the truth so he will have an excuse to tag along too. He will be watching us like a hawk tonight so be careful what you say to Ruby and the President."

"So you think we should just give up then, do you Lizzie?" Ben replied.

"No, I'm saying we need to make our way to Area 51 then persuade Robert Jenkins-Smyth to let us finish what we started," Lizzie reiterated. "This is my first mission and will be my last if we go back empty handed or disobey orders. We also need the expertise of John Briggs and his team."

"Ok Lizzie you have obviously thought this through in great detail." Ben said. "So, this will be plan C then."

"Is that not why you asked for my help on this mission?" Lizzie said with a cheeky grin. She knew Ben fancied her and couldn't resist teasing him a bit. "I need to get ready, the Limo will be here soon." Lizzie rushed into the bedroom taking all hers bags with her.

When Lizzie emerged from the bedroom a little later, Ben just stared at her with his jaw dropped. Lizzie was wearing a full-length black silk evening gown with sparkling sequins, that had been adjusted in no time to fit her like a glove, clearly showing her slim figure. Accessorised with a black designer clutch bag and black stiletto heels, with a hint of red shining from the soles. Enhanced by the most amazing diamond necklace with matching earrings (these were only on loan from Tiffany's), the whole effect was that Lizzie sparkled like the entire universe of stars. *She was even more beautiful than before if that was at all possible,* Ben thought.

"Wow" he heard himself say. "I mean you look stunning," he quickly corrected himself, closing his mouth but continuing to stare.

"Thank you," a slightly embarrassed but very smiley Lizzie replied. She liked dressing up for special occasions but had not done so for a while, so it felt fantastic to have this beautiful dress and dripping with these amazing and very expensive diamonds. Good job they would be protected by the US secret service. Also, she was flattered by Ben's reaction.

Ben informed agent Walker that they were both ready now. he was outside their room, as usual accompanied by Agent Brad Stringer. Both had changed into dinner suits and would be escorting them on the short drive down Pennsylvania Avenue to the White House. Ben and Lizzie were after all guests of honour to the President of the United States of America.

It was so surreal to both Ben and Lizzie. As they approached the entrance to the White House, they were welcomed in by the security guards and then drove the few hundred yards up the main entrance. As the doors of the limo opened, and the sheer vastness of the White House stood before them, Ben turned to Lizzie and said, "let's show them how the Brits party."

Lizzie blushed, giving Ben the unimpressed-wife-look again,

"Just relax, Ben" she said, "and be yourself", as she noticed him getting a bit nervous. "You don't want your heart racing, do you?", squeezing his hand a little in an affectionate way, as if to say *I'll be here to look after you.*

He smiled back at Lizzie and mouthed a thank you.

When Ben and Lizzie entered the great banqueting room that had seen so many famous gatherings, they were introduced to the gathered dignitaries. Standing in the far end of this vast room was Ruby with her mother and father either side, all three sporting enormous grins.

"Ruby looks lovely Lizzie" said to Ben, and he nodded, then looked at Lizzie, who was the best-looking girl in the room by a country mile.

After they were formally introduced to President Carlsen, he personally thanked Ben for saving his daughter and said Ben would receive the highest bravery award offered to non-Americans.

This made Ben blush a little, but he had to stay as calm as he could, because if he disappeared in this company, he would never get back home to England, let alone anywhere near Area 51.

Ben was seated on the right of President Carlsen, with Ruby on Ben's right. Lizzie was next to the First Lady and had Agent Brad Stringer on her left. At least Lizzie had an ally in the First Lady, they had spent most of the previous night talking and watching Ben and Ruby dance.

Lizzie noticed something very odd about the formal layout of the large banqueting table. There were bottles of burger sauce and ketchup set out at equal distances.

President Carlsen stood and thanked everyone for changing their plans at very short notice but hoped they understood the special reasons why they were here this evening. President Carlsen then turned to Ben and publicly thanked him from the bottom of his heart, as a father first and a President second, for being really brave and risking his own life to save a stranger.

"So, can you all please be upstanding as I propose a toast to Benedict Norton and his girlfriend Lizzie Summer." After the toast, a huge round of applause rung out, started by Ruby Carlsen.

Just then, an army of identically dressed waiters started to serve the food. This made Ben blush again, at the burgers and fries (as the British find out to their horror, when in America you get crisps if you order chips). Laughter then rang out from the seated dignitaries. Ben's favourite food was announced by the Master of Ceremonies.

Ben, Ruby and Lizzie got milk shakes instead of alcohol as they were under-age. This made Lizzie feel like a young child. She turned to the First Lady and asked if they ever allowed Ruby to drink alcohol, as Lizzie's parents often gave her the smallest glass (not much larger than thimble) of wine at Christmas and New Year, and she could identify the good stuff from the plonk at a very early age, even turning down a glass of red wine she had had on the 2nd of January saying she wanted the wine from the previous evening).

"Never outside of our private quarters," the First Lady replied. "When you are in the public eye as much as we are you can't take the risks of it getting into the papers. The President would lose millions of voters. At the moment," continued the first lady, "she doesn't appear interested in alcohol. Only boys, so sorry if she is paying Ben more attention than she should but it is clear even to Ruby he only has eyes for you, Lizzie."

Lizzie smiled at the First Lady, but was still a little jealous deep down of Ruby because she was by far getting more attention than Lizzie since they had arrived in Washington.

Ben spent most of the evening talking with President Carlsen. This did not please Ruby very much but she could not show it as he was the guest of honour and Ruby had quickly learnt since her father had become President, everything gets noticed in the White House and ends up in the papers, so she has been lectured enough times about behaving and not embarrassing her father. Ben was amazed the president had heard of his father and was very interested in Professor Norton's, work asking Ben lots of questions about what his father is currently working on. Ben never knew much about the professor's work; it wasn't something

Ben was very interested in, which always annoyed his father. Ben up until recently had not decided what he was going to study at university if he got the grades. But now this had changed, all he wanted to be was a spy working for MI6.

Ben did exchange phone numbers with Ruby and promised to keep in touch, only as friends he had decided, but did not have the heart to disappoint Ruby and tell her that night.

To Brad Stringer's relief and pleasure the evening went without a hitch. No attempts on the President or any of his family. He even found himself starting to like these two British kids. As he assisted Agent Walker in returning their two guests back to their hotel room, he gasped at the request Ben had made in the limo about where they wanted to go tomorrow and continue their vacation.

"Why in god's earth" Brad Stringer said with total puzzlement do you want to go to Area 51? It's a restricted air force base not a tourist attraction!"

"I have always been very interested in Area 51" Ben said, "since I read about Roswell and all the stories about UFO's. Just going there and taking in the atmosphere will be enough."

"Unless you can arrange for a guided tour for us" Lizzie interrupted, "I'm sure the President would be grateful. He did say as we were leaving the White House if he could arrange any VIP visits anywhere, he would."

"Even the President doesn't get guided tours of Area 51," Brad snapped back. "I think he meant the Grand Canyon or Mount Rushmore or even Disney but definitely not Area 51. Anyway, all those reports about UFO's are just that: stories and conspiracy theorists trying to keep their blog numbers up."

"Ok, thanks" said Lizzie, "just return us to Nevada and we will continue our holiday by ourselves. We will hire a car and continue our trip as planned."

"Does that mean you are going to drive to Area 51?" Brad asked?

"Is it Ok if we just drive past and take a few pictures of the countryside," Ben asked.

"No, it's a military base, you can't take any pictures," Brad said, slightly raising his voice. He was starting to suspect these two all over again. *What was around Area 51 that was so important to these two kids that they won't ease off?* He knew they would not get inside, that feat had never been achieved yet, so what were they up to?

The rest of the journey was made in silence; it was late, and it had been a very long day for all of them.

As Agent Walker was closing the hotel suite door, he turned to Ben and informed him that the limo will be ready at about midday to take them to the airport where Airforce 1 would then take them back to Las Vegas as requested.

"Good night sir, sleep well." Agent Walker said as he closed the door behind him. Agent Walker heard the loud music go on as he had the night before just as he took his nightly seat outside the hotel suite door. He would be replaced soon so he could go home and have some sleep before he was due to return the next morning. Ben and Lizzie would think he had been there all night as usual. *Nice kids* he thought to himself, *yep, nice kids.*

Brad Stringer was standing just outside the hotel suite door engrossed in a really interesting phone call.

"Two nuns you say?" Brad said back. After several "ahum"s and "yep"s, he hung up the phone. Brad walked to the end of the hotel corridor signalling that agent Walker should follow him. "They are not to leave your sight tomorrow, Agent Walker. You are to fly with them to Nevada and escort them to their hire car, and a surveillance team will take over."

"Am I allowed to know why we are breaking our promise to them about continuing their vacation alone? Agent Walker enquired.

"Two nuns were seen exiting the 'Security Only' section of McCarran airport, where the CCTV recordings were tampered with," Brad replied. "The nuns had said they had got lost and took a wrong turn. These two nuns were on the same flight from London Heathrow that Ben and Lizzie were on. The two nuns were travelling under false passports. Do you believe in coincidences, Agent Walker, because I sure don't. I knew these two kids were involved somehow and I'm going to get to the bottom of it."

"Yes, Sir" replied Agent Walker, as he returned to his seat outside the hotel suite. *They seem such nice kids to me,* he thought, *just shows you that you can never tell with people these days.*

TWENTY-TWO

As the limo stopped outside the car hire office at McCarran International Airport, Agent Walker rushed around to open the door for Lizzie and Ben.

"I could really get used to travelling like this all the time. It's great," Ben said, as he felt the warm evening desert air hit his face. Meanwhile the driver had opened the boot and was unloading their luggage which had more than doubled since they first arrived in America.

"Unless you have millions stashed away that you haven't told me about, Ben," Lizzie remarked. "This is where the VIP treatment ends for us," as she exited the car and turned to face Agent Walker. "Thank you for looking after us these last couple of days, you are so dedicated to your job."

"My job and my country," Agent Walker replied. "It's been a pleasure knowing you both. Please stay safe and enjoy your vacation."

Agent Walker got back into the limo, and it drove off back to where Airforce One was waiting. He was hoping that Agent Stringer was wrong about these two Brits; he really liked them and found it hard to believe that they would harm anyone, let alone Ruby.

After a couple of minutes of paperwork, Lizzie and Ben were taken to their car and loaded their entire luggage into the vast boot. Lizzie had only had a driving licence a couple of years but had never driven abroad, let alone on the other side of the road.

Ben was studying a large map of Nevada, very carefully working out their route.

"We have to head over to Groom Lake Road which runs through a pass called Jumbled Hills this is where we pass a security checkpoint," Ben told Lizzie. He stopped talking. It was obvious she was not listening to anything he was saying. "What's wrong, Lizzie," Ben enquired.

"I'm fine," Lizzie replied, "just thought getting the car was too quick and easy. Somethings not quite right, it's all been too easy. We must stay alert and get in touch with London."

"Is that why you insisted on this car, rather than the red one they had ready for us?" Ben asked.

"Just being careful," Lizzie replied, "they can't bug every car or put a tracker on all of them, can they?"

"Groom Lake Road, through Jumbled Hill Pass, through the security checkpoint, then what?" Lizzie asked.

"We then descend eastwards to the floor of the Tikaboo Valley leading to State Route 375 also known as Extraterrestrial Highway. What great names!" Ben said. "I didn't know this place was so big either," he continued. "60 square miles of top-secret base. How do they keep people out?"

"With the very latest technology is my guess" Lizzie replied.

"Maybe," Ben reiterated but they haven't come up against Superhero Benedict Norton yet have they!"

Lizzie laughed out loud.

"Do you like that title, Ben, because it's so bad. Next you'll be telling me you have a cape!"

"Well, if you think it's bad," a blushing Ben said, "I won't use it again, I promise you Lizzie. A cape? Never. It's so uncool."

"We need to find a motel for the night and set off in the morning, before we unleash Superhero Benedict Norton on Area 51" Lizzie interrupted struggling not to burst out laughing.

"I thought we agreed not to use that name again," Ben said, feeling very embarrassed.

"I won't mention it again" Lizzie said, still smiling and trying not to laugh.

It didn't take long for them to find a motel and check in. On entering the motel room Ben was at first a little disappointed that there were two single beds, then thought this was better as it was becoming more and more difficult to stop his pulse racing when he was lying next to Lizzie. He thought she was so beautiful, brave, and clever, and was falling for her in a very big way.

"This is what they call a suite around here. It's a bit smaller than we have been used to." Ben said jokingly, "but it will have to do."

Lizzie smiled; Ben made her laugh with his silly Dad jokes, as she called them.

"I need to contact London, Ben, to try to convince them we should carry on." Lizzie said. "Lock the door behind me and don't let anyone in."

"Yes, Dear," Ben said sarcastically.

"Is that what you think of me, as your bossy wife?" Lizzie said. "I'm only trying to keep you safe, *both* of us safe."

"What can they do to me Lizzie, kill me again?" Ben said. "You are the one who needs to be careful. I'll be fine; you go and get London to let us continue. Sorry if I offended you, I always turn to humour when I'm nervous."

Lizzie left and made her way to the motel diner, where she was told there was a payphone they could use to phone home. She had been gone quite a while and Ben was now wondering that this could all be over before the real job had started. If Lizzie could not persuade Robert Jenkins-Smyth, they would be on the next flight back to London. Saving Ruby had really messed things up, but he would do it again if need be.

When Lizzie returned all glum faced, Ben knew it was all over.

"Well, when do we fly back home then?" Ben asked.

"It's not that simple," Lizzie replied, going straight over to the TV remote and putting the volume up high. "London wants us to continue to Area 51 and locate the gun," she whispered. "And to make matters worse, they also say we have a full American surveillance team monitoring our every move."

"How do they know that? Ben asked, trying not to speak too loudly.

"Because" Lizzie continued, "MI6 has a team watching the American team that are watching us."

"And they still want us to proceed to Area 51? That's crazy" Ben stated. "They can't hurt me, but I won't allow them to put your life in danger. I'm going to speak to Robert Jenkins-Smyth myself."

"Calm down, Ben," Lizzie said. "That's really kind of you to care about me, but I knew when I volunteered what I was letting myself in for." Lizzie gave Ben a gentle squeeze on both arms. "That's really sweet you care so much for me, but I will be fine Ben; you will make sure of that won't you."

Ben replied with a low muffled yes. "Of course, I'll take care of you" he said. What he wanted to say was that he loved her, but he had never said that to anyone before, not even to his mother who had died when he was only five.

"I will have to come up with a plan C, then" Ben said, "as we are being followed."

"No, we have already discarded C, Ben, its plan D now." Lizzie replied.

"It will be plan Z by the time we pull this off," Ben mumbled to himself, "if we ever pull this off." *Why would London risk the Americans getting me? Ben thought, that's the last thing they would want. What is going on?*

Ben and Lizzie set off the next day but not until they had given their car a thorough check to see if it had been tampered with.

Originally Ben had agreed to take the first shift of two hours keeping an eye on the hire car parked outside their motel room but had fallen asleep after only a few minutes.

"It's very tiring just staring out into the darkness at a motionless car" he said to Lizzie when she found him sleeping. After that, there was no point in maintaining the vigil as the car could have been tampered with already. They both decided to get a good night's sleep and check the car in the morning.

As neither knew what they were looking for this didn't take very long. Back in the motel room, they were finalising their plan to get Ben inside Area 51. They had also agreed not to speak in the car but to pass each other notes and see if they could spot the surveillance team. Nervously they set off on what was going to be the most defining day of this mission and quite possibly of their entire lives.

The first test was going to be getting past the security checkpoint on Groom Lake Road.

As the car approached Ben started to get nervous and was struggling to keep his pulse rate down. Since the kidnapping of Ruby, they had been closely watched and Ben had not disappeared once so was a little out of practice in controlling his heart rate.

Ben managed to keep it together and after a couple of mundane questions at the security checkpoint, "Where are you heading?" and "What are you doing out here?", they were soon sent on their way.

"That was easy" a very relieved Ben said to Lizzie.

"Yes, too easy" Lizzie replied. "I don't like this, I don't like how easy this is going so far."

"You're getting paranoid Lizzie," Ben said. "We are just a couple of kids on vacation to them, why would they give us a hard time?"

"Maybe you're right Ben, maybe you're right." Lizzie repeated.

They were both getting very nervous. Their plan to write things down and not speak had also been forgotten by Ben so Lizzie gave up too.

The two had not spotted anyone following the whole day.

"Both surveillance teams are very good" Ben said, looking around outside.

Lizzie turned to Ben in the passenger seat.

"Are you ready? It's time," she said. "Have you come up with plan D yet?"

"No, I'm going to have to play it by ear, go inside, locate the gun and see if there are any weaknesses to their security, we can exploit using my skills."

"That sounds like a good plan to me," Lizzie said, trying to reassure Ben.

"I'm ready" Ben replied. He was getting very nervous so it shouldn't be too difficult to disappear and stay invisible throughout his time over the fence. Ben climbed into the back seat and made out he was lying down, all so whoever was watching them could not see him actually disappear.

Lizzie had come to a stop near the perimeter fence of Area 51, turned to face an empty back seat and said in a very quiet soft voice "Good luck Ben and be careful please."

She waited a couple of minutes to be sure Ben was out whilst checking the three vehicles that passed. She didn't recognise any of the faces, so she thought all was going to plan. It's all up to Ben now.

Ben was floating invisibly towards the base. He turned to give a final glance at Lizzie who was just pulling off and making her way to find another motel and wait. She was due to return in three hours, enough time, they both thought to locate the gun. All Ben had to do was stay invisible for three hours. No problem, Ben thought to himself very unconvincingly.

Back in London, Ben had been briefed about some of the layout and security. He knew as long as he stayed invisible, he would be fine. If he were to reappear, he could trigger one of the numerous buried motion sensors or worse, be seen on one of the many security cameras. He headed for the centre of the complex as he thought that would be the most secure area and where they would keep their most secret research facilities.

That's it! he thought to himself. He saw a sign that read Foreign Technology Division. FTD. *I'll start in there*, as he floated through the wall. It was early afternoon now and the place was busy with people in white coats moving about. He had to be very careful not to relax too much as he would then reappear, and that would take some explaining, he thought. "So, what are you doing, young man naked in the most secure building in the USA?" Would be the first question. They would then put him in a strait jacket, lock him up and throw away the key. "Sunbathing" was his favourite reply he had prepared just in case.

Ben spent the next 20 minutes weaving his way from room to room bypassing all the security doors and cameras with ease.

Making his way down to the basement level he entered a large room full of electronic equipment the likes of which he had never seen before, even after spending the last ten years visiting his father in labs. On a bench in the middle of this room surrounded by four men and two women was the gun. It was exactly the same as the one Ratzilla had used on him. He stayed in the room and listened to the scientists discussing the tests they had run and were going to run next.

There was an elegant lady in her early forties that appeared to Ben to be the lead scientist and was asking the most probing questions. It turned out that she was the head of FTD and lead scientist advisor to the White house,

Professor Marie Antony, the only scientist to have a dual degree from MIT, but also a double first from Cambridge.

"So, tomorrow when I make my report to President Carlsen, I am to inform him that the five brightest scientists in the whole of America have, after seven days, failed to discover absolutely anything about this weapon?! Not even the sub alloy used, where it was made, how the weapon fires, nothing?"

A bespectacled man interrupted and said that the only person who had previously been able to fire the gun was now dead. He had been shot by the police during his last robbery attempt. This is when the gun came into the possession of the authorities.

"We have tried using his dead body and now his amputated hand, but the gun still won't work." another white coat said.

Oh wow, Ben thought to himself, *they've chopped this poor man's hand off and still it won't work. What the hell would they do to me if they catch me and get me drugged up?*

"So," said Professor Antony, "to summarise. The gun then is not of a technology any of us has come across before, not of any sub alloy known to us. So, where did it come from and how did Connor Jackson get hold of it and make it work? Questions, questions, and more questions, but no answers. It will surely be a very brief meeting with President Carlsen tomorrow unless you give me something. Have you heard anything from the CIA regarding the British incident? Is that the same gun?" Professor Antony continued.

"The Brits have lost their gun and the shooter. A manhunt has been launched but to our knowledge neither has been found yet" said another of the white coats. "The

British also know nothing about the technology, our sources inform us."

What sources? Ben thought, *we have a leak back at MI6. Do they know about me? Surely, they must, if they know all about the gun Ratzilla had.* There were now a million things going through Ben's mind. *Is Lizzie in danger?* he wondered. *Lizzie said she thought something was not right about all of this but what. I need to get back to the perimeter fence and warn Lizzie.* Just as Ben was about to leave, the scientists meeting finished, and they disbursed, leaving the gun unattended on the bench. Looking around, there were cameras everywhere, so he could not reappear and take the gun. *How can I get it out? I would have to appear to pick it up but then once I disappear the gun would just fall to the ground.* Ben decided to hang around a little longer and see where the gun was kept. He would have to return tonight and take it then. He would work out how later with Lizzie's help.

The scientists were starting to pack up their things and clearing their own rubbish, putting it into a large bin near the door. *That's it!* Ben thought, *of course they don't have regular cleaners, this place is so top secret the scientists clean up themselves. If I can get the gun into the bin without being spotted then follow it until its outside the base, I will have stolen the most valuable possession from the most secure installation in America! We now have plan E. Lizzie will be so impressed when I turn up with the gun and so will everyone back in London.*

Ben spotted a spare white coat hanging on a hook about ten feet from the gun. *If I can grab that quickly, put it on, then move the gun to the bin and disappear again, nobody will be any the wiser. Just a white coat on the floor. But I must do this just as the last person is about to leave, otherwise they will see the gun is missing and sound the alarm shutting this place down.*

Ben thought he had enough time to go to the meeting point at the perimeter fence, tell Lizzie what he had planned, and then return and wait until the last man was about to leave. Ben was so happy with himself he nearly reappeared unintentionally. *That would have blown it,* he thought, *and I would be a laughingstock back at MI6 and worst of all what would Lizzie think of me then?*

Convinced his plan E was fool proof, he made his way back to the fence to meet with Lizzie. Ben noticed the hire car waiting at exactly the right location with Lizzie sitting patiently inside. He floated inside the vehicle behind the driver and quickly got dressed again. Lizzie was relieved he was back, safe and in one piece. As they were sitting in the hire car Ben brought Lizzie up to date with what he had seen and heard. He then started to tell her all about plan E.

"But Ben," Lizzie said, "our mission was only to locate the gun, not steal it. If we get caught, it would create an almighty rift between Britain and America."

"I overheard Robert Jenkins-Smyth tell Briggs that they wanted the gun," Ben said. "This mission was not about just finding it, they already knew it was here. MI6 wants the technology; the Americans are no closer to working the gun out, so if we take it back, we could try to make it work. We have the best scientists in the world; I know that because my father is one of them."

"But if the Americans find out we have taken it, this could cause serious problems between our countries," Lizzie replied. "And Ben, don't forget we are under surveillance, stealing the gun from Area 51 would be nearly impossible on its own but with the security service watching it is impossible, even with your powers. We will have to get the go ahead from London before I can let you go back."

"Ok Lizzie, we will do it your way," Ben reluctantly agreed.

Lizzie had also managed to find a motel to the south of Area 51 which meant they did not have to keep going through the security checkpoint arousing suspicion every time. As soon as they arrived back, Lizzie went to the payphone and rang London.

Lizzie returned a few minutes later, the colour completely drained from her face.

"Robert Jenkins-Smyth has given us orders to steal the gun tonight," Lizzie said as she slumped on the bed. "But why would he risk, at best, our two countries special relationship, or even worse the possibility of war between us. What have we started Ben?"

"Do you think Robert Jenkins-Smyth could be a double agent?" Ben asked. "After all I did overhear things from the lab that referred to the American's sources. This mission and the gun were supposed to be top, top secret."

"No, I don't think so," Lizzie replied. "Why would the Americans steal it from themselves, no, he definitely is not working for America. Robert Jenkins-Smyth has more than once risked his life for his country. We have our sources and I'm sure the Americans have theirs. No, there is more to this than we have been told. Do you think you can get the gun into the bin without being spotted by the cameras?"

"No not definitely," Ben said, "but if I cover my face with the white coat, they won't know who it was that took the gun and placed it in the bin. Surely they can't be watching live every camera all the time? There are hundreds if not thousands of cameras in that place. I'm sure we will be long gone by the time they check the CCTV and see someone wearing a white coat steal their gun."

TWENTY-THREE

Lizzie drove Ben back to Area 51 and as before, Ben went over onto the back seat to disappear just in case someone was still watching. Both Lizzie and Ben had been extra vigilant, but still could not see anyone following them.

"They are good, both the surveillance teams, very good indeed," both Lizzie and Ben said. Lizzie stopped the car in a different spot from before, thinking this would be less likely to draw attention to what they were up to.

Ben disappeared just as Lizzie was telling him to be careful. A few minutes later he was floating through the walls of the FTD building and heading down to the basement level where the gun was. As he entered the lab, he could see three scientists huddled around the bench where the gun had been a little earlier. Ben went over but they were not looking at the gun. In fact, it was not on the bench at all. *Where could it be?* he thought, as he flew around the lab in search of his prize.

Just then, the three men walked to the door, turned out all the lights except a security light, and left the lab, shutting the door behind them. The bin had also gone. *This is not good,* Ben thought, *not good at all. Time for plan F,* he thought, but as there wasn't a plan E anymore, he would have to come up with something now, and fast.

"Think, Ben" he said to himself. "What would James Bond do. James Bond would find the gun and shoot his way out. But I'm not Bond and this is America, and they all have guns here, so I can't shoot my way out. Come on Ben stop thinking about films and find the gun." Ben knew he could not reappear and physically check all the draws because he would be spotted on one of the cameras. At the end of the Lab was a door that looked like a broom cupboard. Ben floated through the door and to his relief found there were no cameras visible, only some spare white coats and an umbrella. *Who would need an umbrella in the middle of the desert?* he thought, *can't be because of all the rain they get, more likely to keep the sun off their head.* He decided to reappear, put on the coat, and use the umbrella to cover his face and his identity. Ben got dressed and opened the umbrella, even though it is bad luck indoors, and re-entered the lab. If someone were watching this lab on one of the cameras, all hell would let loose. *Right,* he thought, *where would you store something as precious as this gun. Either locked away somewhere secure or in plain sight of the cameras.* Ben started opening every draw or cupboard that was big enough to hold the gun. Twenty minutes later he still hadn't found the gun. Just as he was thinking about giving up, he decided to get a cold drink for himself. This spy stuff was thirsty work. Ben opened the fridge door next to the coffee machine to see what drinks they had and there, sitting on the top shelf, was the gun. *Why would they put it in the fridge? Were they worried it would go off? Overheat or something maybe.*

Ben removed it, and went over to the door, still holding the umbrella up and covering the gun from the cameras. Just by the door was a small empty box and some other bits of rubbish. The box was big enough to take the gun. Ben had an idea. He put the gun in the box and carried it to the cupboard. Inside, he found some tape and a marker. He wrote something on the box, then took it back to the door and put it down where he found it. Ben returned to the cupboard and replaced the coat and umbrella. He then heard someone returning to the lab. *Quick!* he thought, *I'd better disappear again and see who that is.*

Ben floated through the cupboard door as soon as he could and to his surprise, it was a security guard taking the rubbish out and the box, dumping them into a large trolley. His plan F might still work after all.

Ben followed the guard upstairs and from room to room he collected all the rubbish and threw them into the trolley. By now the box was covered in lots of other boxes and bags of rubbish. Soon the guard had collected all the rubbish and was heading out of the FTD building towards a much smaller outbuilding with a very large steel pipe protruding from the roof. The sign outside read Incinerator.

Oh no! Ben thought, *they are going to burn it!* Ben followed the guards every move and into the small outbuilding. Once at the incinerator, the guard started unloading the rubbish and throwing it into the blazing hot furnace. When he pulled the small box out of the trolley, he went to throw it in but noticed Ben's writing on the box. TOXIC WASTE.

"What are they doing putting toxic waste in with the trash?" the guard said out loud. "They should know better being scientists as well." The guard put the box down by the door to remove it later when he had finished his shift. "I need to ask for a raise if they want me to get rid of toxic waste" he mumbled to himself. Once the guard had emptied the trolley, he wheeled it out and headed to the next building.

Ben reappeared, scratching his head. *How can I get this off the base without getting seen?* Then he heard the noise of a helicopter engine starting up. He found an old boiler suit and quickly put it on, then picking up the box, he sneaked outside, taking care not to be seen. The helicopter was about 50 meters away; it was a small four seater. *I can run get on board with the box then disappear, once back on the ground I can get in touch with Lizzie and she can come and pick me up. Great!* Ben thought. As he approached the helicopter, the pilot was busy checking the main fuselage and exterior parts of the helicopter. Then the pilot suddenly stopped and was now staring at something. Ben turned to look.

There was purple smoke outside the FTD building. *Probably an experiment gone wrong,* Ben thought to himself, continuing stealthily to make his way to the helicopter before the pilot could notice him. *I can sneak in now while the pilot is still distracted.* Ben climbed on board and placed the box under one of the rear seats and quickly vanished. The pilot got back inside and made contact with the tower to get clearance to take off. Thankfully, thought Ben, he hadn't noticed the old boiler suite on the back seat. It wasn't long before they were on their way up and away from the most secure base in America. Although it was very dark outside, Ben could make out in the distance the unmistakable sight of the night sky above Las Vegas. This tunnel of light could be seen for miles.

A little while later ,the pilot was seeking permission to land at McCarran International Airport. *He must be going there to pick up an important military person*, Ben thought. After they landed, the pilot made his way into an office. Ben seized on this chance to reappear, get dressed, and leave with the box. He was still in a secure area of the airport and after last weeks attempted kidnapping, security had been stepped up even more. Ben noticed an empty, large, stretch limo parked outside a hanger. *If I can hide the box in that then follow it, I'm home free.* Ben sneaked up behind the limo, opened the boot and pushed the box to the back of the empty boot, quietly closing it again. He went to the rear of the hanger and disappeared, then made his way back to the limo and floated into the closed boot. A few minutes later he heard noises and the boot opening.

"Don't put that in the trunk" he heard a man say "I want it with me at all times." Soon the limo was on its way. Ben floated into the Limo to see who it was that was helping him. Once inside he saw a young man dressed in black leathers, *Wow!* Ben thought, *it's Rick Dark, the lead singer and guitarist of The Greatest. I would love to get his autograph, but I think he would freak out if I just reappeared next to him naked. That would give him a great story to tell when he went onto a chat show to promote the bands next album:*

'I was in my limo man just chilling out on my way to my hotel, man, when this English dude just appears next to me, completely naked, man, and asks me for my autograph. I said how about a selfie, dude, but he refused because he had no clothes on, then he just disappears again, man, surreal. I haven't had a drink or taken any drugs since, man.'

Ben loved the band but could not risk the mission just for an autograph or a selfie. Rick Dark had a large guitar case sitting right next to him and a small leather bag. *He travelled very light,* Ben thought.

The limo went through security without any problems, Ben thought he must be a regular here, and drove straight out of the airport into Las Vegas. It soon pulled up outside the Mirage hotel. The pop star got out and the driver took the one small piece of luggage and the guitar case with him.

"That's all there is", the driver said to the hotel porter as he was about to open the trunk.

The limo, with Ben still hiding in the back, pulled out of the hotel drive and down the strip. About ten minutes later the driver pulled into a large garage full of gleaming limos. The driver parked up, went to the office, spoke to someone, then said goodnight. *That's all I need,* Ben thought, *an all-night garage,* as he floated around checking where he was and trying to work out how to get the box containing the gun out. Ben decided to hide in the boot and get some rest and wait until it closed for the night and the staff went home. Ben was also so tired; he needed the rest. *This spy stuff is hard work,* he thought. *I hope Lizzie is not too worried, it's been quite a few hours since I left her.* Ben then dozed off; he was awoken by the sound of a large metal shutter being pulled down to the floor. *Great,* he thought, *they have finally closed.* Ben floated out of the boot and looked around to make sure the coast was clear; he also found some dirty mechanic's overalls. Ben re-appeared and quickly slipped on the dirty overalls, then made his way to the boot of the limo. Suddenly, there was an almighty noise like an alarm siren. It was quite deafening as he opened the limo boot to take out the box. He must have set the alarm off. *That's funny,* he thought, smiling. *I get in and out of area 51 undetected but I get caught in a garage.* He gets the box and runs towards the rear where there is an emergency exit; he just manages to get out when the police arrive outside to check out the alarm. *That was close,* he thought, *very close.*

Ben is now walking somewhere in Las Vegas barefoot and carrying a box that says toxic waste, which has inside it a gun.

"Great" he says to himself. "The things I do for my country. I need to contact Lizzie straight away." A little further down the street Ben saw a clothes shop. He went round the back, disappeared once more, and entered hoping this time not to set the alarm off. He made his way into the rear office and re-appeared. *I must ring the motel immediately*; Ben rang the motel and asked for their room and was put through straight away.

"Hi Lizzie, I've done it, no, *we've* done it, but not quite to plan" Ben said. "I'm on plan F, in fact and it's working so far.

"I've been worried sick" Lizzie said. "I waited and waited for hours, outside that base, every time a car went by, I thought I was about to be arrested. Where are you, are you safe?"

It sounded to Ben that she had been crying.

"I'm fine" he said. "It's been a very long night, but I have Uncle Roberts present. I'm in Las Vegas, can you pick me up please?"

"In Las Vegas?" Lizzie repeated. "How did you get there? Never mind," she said, "you can tell me all when I pick you up. Where are you?"

"I'm borrowing some clothes from a shop then I will make my way to the Mirage hotel, it's a large hotel on the strip. Next to Caesars Palace. The lead guitarist from The Greatest is staying there, so it must be nice."

"Ok", Lizzie said, "I will be with you as soon as I can. See you at the Mirage Hotel."

Ben picked out some casual clothes and a small holdall for the gun. He made a note of all the prices so he would pay the owner back for what he borrowed; his conscience would allow him to steal a top-secret gun from the American Government but not steal from some small shop owner. Ben left through the back door and took the gun out of the box marked toxic waste which was hidden in the back yard. This time thankfully not setting any alarms off.

After wandering around for a while, Ben found the Mirage hotel and entered into the reception area, where there was the largest fish tank he had ever seen. He could not help but stare at all the fish that it contained, even sharks.

It was about 8am by the time Lizzie arrived at the hotel. She ran at Ben as soon as she saw him and gave him a big hug. Ben thought she was going to kiss him, but she pulled away, wiping a tear from beneath her eye, and without warning, Lizzie hit him on the chest as hard as she could.

"You scared me so much last night! Maybe I'm not cut out for field work after all" Lizzie said. "Maybe I should just go back to London, nice and safe, that will do for me."

"I'm so sorry, Lizzie, but nothing went to plan." Ben replied. "Without your calmness and intellect, we would not have pulled this off. I could not have done this alone. You are a great field operative."

"London has instructed us to take a room here for today while they get us some support." Lizzie interrupted. "You can tell me everything once we are in the hotel room with the door locked. We don't know who might be listening. Is it in there?" Lizzie pointed to the small bag.

"Yes" replied a smiling Ben. "It sure is."

After checking in, they made their way up to their suite. There were no rooms available, just the honeymoon suite. The cost didn't matter as London was paying and they had both got quite used to travelling in style. They just dumped their bags in the bedroom, and both sat on the giant bed staring at each other.

"We did it!" Ben yelled, "We did it, young lady!"

With that, Lizzie punched Ben as hard as she could, sending him sprawling to the floor.

"I've been called young lady for the last time," Lizzie said.

Ben picked himself up and looked at Lizzie, then smiled at her.

"I deserved that" Ben said. "Where did you learn to punch like that?" Ben enquired.

"I learn everything quickly," Lizzie answered, "so don't forget that."

Before Ben could even start to tell Lizzie what he had been through, there was a knock on the hotel room door.

"Room service" a voice called out. "A bottle of the hotels finest Champagne with our compliments from the manager on your arrival at the Mirage, Sir and Madam."

Wow, Ben thought. *That was quick, now that's what I call service.* Lizzie started to walk from the bedroom and towards the main door, and without thinking of checking, Lizzie opened the door and froze for a second, stunned by what she was looking at, or more to the point, who she was looking at. Confronted by Robert Jenkins-Smyth and Agent Brad Stringer together, Lizzie then composed herself and screamed at Ben. "Disappear Ben! Save yourself!"

TWENTY-FOUR

Ben could not leave Lizzie to deal with all this by herself, as he had followed her to the main hotel room door. But he was not going to let them get the gun either without putting up a fight. Ben disappeared, leaving his new clothes in a pile on the floor, and quickly made his way into the bedroom. He re-appeared, grabbed the holdall containing the gun, and then hid it under the bed. It was the only place he could think of in that short space of time. Ben then ran to the bathroom and took one of the hotel bath robes, put it on, and walked back out to where Lizzie was being questioned by Robert Jenkins-Smyth and Agent Brad Stringer.

"Ah, there you are Ben, I'm glad you saw sense and returned," Jenkins-Smyth remarked. "We have a bit of explaining to do, well quite a bit really. But most importantly, we are all in this together," he continued.

Ben glanced at Lizzie, then returned his gaze to Jenkins-Smyth. "What do you mean, we are all in this together?" an angry Ben enquired.

"Please Ben, just calm down and we will explain

everything to you and Lizzie. We owe you that much at least," Brad Stringer interrupted.

"Are you both working together? Which side are you on?" Ben asked. "Which side are Lizzie and I working for?"

"Ben, just sit down and stay calm" Jenkins-Smyth interrupted.

Ben walked over to Lizzie and sat down next to her.

"Ok" Ben said. "Please tell us what is going on."

Robert Jenkins-Smyth sat opposite Lizzie and Ben while Brad Stringer remained standing.

"I'm sorry but I haven't been quite honest with you both Jenkins-Smyth started. "The special relationship that Britain and America have has withstood two world wars and the cold war. So, I'm afraid nothing can be allowed to happen that might break that relationship or even put it in danger. I had no choice but to inform my counterpart in the CIA of your mission. It was mutually agreed that we would let you continue."

"What was the point of continuing if the Americans were in on it?" Lizzie asked. "They could just let you have the gun, or you could share the technology."

"Well, it's not just about the gun," Jenkins-Smyth replied. "The CIA wanted to test the security at Area 51, and we both wanted to see what could be achieved by Ben using his new powers. This was a good opportunity for both sides to put a lot of their untested skills and security systems to the test. Which, thanks to you both, we have just done."

"So, this has all just been a security exercise?" Ben said.

"No, far more than that" Jenkins-Smyth said. "Up until the kidnapping of Ruby Carlsen, only Home Secretary

Adams and the head of the CIA knew what was going on. But we had no choice but to inform President Carlsen that your intervention at McCarran airport was purely coincidental. You were, as they say, at the right place at the right time to save Ruby. So, if nothing else, you stopped a major terrorist attack from being successful, and saved Ruby Carlsen's life."

"I knew there was more to your involvement with the kidnapping than you were both letting on, but I kept on getting the brush off even from President Carlsen who tried to get me to back off," Agent Brad Stringer interrupted. "I was only informed of your involvement and mission yesterday when I was about to arrest you both for being at Area 51, against my insistence to stay away."

"How do we know what you are saying is true and you are not both rogue agents working for whoever made the gun in the first place?" Lizzie enquired.

"Don't you worry about that, we will do more than prove we are all together on this soon enough," Brad replied.

Ben proceeded to explain how he managed to remove the gun from Area 51, his helicopter ride, and his time in the boot of the limo.

"Can you get Rick Dark's autograph for me as he's staying at this hotel please?" Ben asked Agent Stringer. "Also, what was happening at the FTD building and all that purple smoke?" Ben asked.

"It's still being investigated" Agent Stringer replied. "It's still a mystery, did you have anything to do with it, was it a diversion you started?"

"No," Ben replied, "it helped me get on board the helicopter, but I had nothing to do with it."

Just then there was a knock on the door. Brad Stringer went over and opened it. To both Lizzie and Ben's surprise, through the door walked President Carlsen, closely followed by a large entourage of secret service agents. One of which was Agent Walker, who smiled at them as soon as he saw them. He always knew they were good kids.

"I hope you are not very angry with us all. Sometimes things happen for a reason," President Carlsen stated. "I will nevertheless be indebted to you both for saving Ruby's life. Have you been briefed with what we require from you now?"

"Not yet sir, we were just about to when you arrived," Brad interrupted, a little nervously.

Whilst Lizzie and Ben were talking to the president, their bedroom was cleared of their belongings, ready to be moved.

"The gun is not here" one of the agents said out loud.

"No, it's under the bed" Ben said. "Sorry but I didn't know what was going on when you first came in, Mr. Jenkins-Smyth, so I hid it. Can I please put some clothes on now if we are being moved?"

"You hid it Ben," President Carlsen said. "Good work, don't trust anyone. That will keep you safe in this business."

"Thank you, Mr. President," Ben sheepishly replied.

"Of course, you can put some clothes on; after all you have done for both our countries. You are not a prisoner, we will be taking you both back to Area 51, but as the guests of the United States Government this time," President Carlsen said.

"Why are we returning to Area 51?" Lizzie asked. "And what is it you still require us to do now?"

"Please be patient, Miss Summer," Robert Jenkins-Smyth said. "We still have many questions to ask you both before we brief you on what is required from you now."

"Can someone please take $327 to Jakes Clothing in Downtown Las Vegas? I borrowed these shoes, clothes and that bag from his shop to enable me to escape the police." Ben asked.

"The secret service can take care of that immediately," President Carlsen stated. "Anything else you require can also be arranged."

"Can someone please get the autograph of Rick Dark, The Greatest lead guitarist please?" Ben asked. "He's staying here at this hotel."

"Yes of course," President Carlsen replied, "and get a signed photo for Ruby too. I want a private word with Ben, please" continued the President to all present in the room.

Robert Jenkins-Smyth turned and gave a quizzical glance at Ben, trying to thought-transfer over to him: *you are British first and foremost. Your loyalties are to your Queen and country.*

Ben saw the look and knew that Jenkins-Smyth was not to be crossed. There would be dire consequences, if not for Ben himself, but for his father and Lizzie.

The president put his arm on Ben's shoulder and walked him away from the hotel room door, out of earshot of Jenkins-Smyth and the secret agents protecting him.

"I know what your mission was and that you saving Ruby was putting that mission in grave danger of failure, but you carried on and saved Ruby's life nevertheless, for which I will always be in your debt. If there is anything you ever need, I will always be there for you. If the Brits don't treat you well, you can come and live here."

"Thank you, Mr President" replied Ben. "I am being very well treated back home and will always call America my second home. You have already been very hospitable to Lizzie and me." *The Americans want me for my powers too,* Ben thought to himself.

Lizzie and Ben were then taken back to Area 51 by military helicopter and whizzed through security like the VIP's they had become. They were both given ten minutes to freshen up, then were taken and seated separately in adjoining interview rooms to be debriefed; this didn't take long for Lizzie as she had been under surveillance the whole time they were on their mission. Ben on the other hand would take much longer to debrief. He was again being watched through a one-way mirror, and Agent Brad Stringer was asking the questions again.

I'd better get used to this treatment, Ben thought. *After all, I am the freak in the room, all the white coats behind that mirror want to analyse everything about me and probably dissect me if they were given the chance to get their hands on me.*

After explaining how he managed to escape Area 51 with the gun into the helicopter, Ben paused and asked Brad if they had uncovered what all that purple smoke was outside the FTD building he had seen.

"No not yet," Agent Stringer replied. "That's another mystery altogether."

"Well, it was very useful because it distracted the helicopter pilot for long enough so I could hide the gun on board and disappear without being noticed," Ben replied.

"At this point, Ben was sure he could sense a lot of activity behind the mirror. So, what or who created that purple smoke he saw last night? Was it another terrorist attack? *This was bad for the Americans,* he thought. *Had someone else tried to steal the gun but he had beaten them to it? That's probably the case, but they must have breached all the bases security systems just to get to the FTD building and let off that purple smoke. No mean feat, unless like me they are invisible…* This made him think maybe others can make themselves invisible. *Maybe it's not just me* he thought. *Robert Jenkins-Smyth was right, far too many questions and no answers* he thought to himself as he looked at the glass wall, wondering what was being said behind it, It was definitely about him, that he was sure of.

"Ok" Brad said to Ben, "so you get into the helicopter then what happened?"

Ben had to go over his story a couple of times before they would let him take a break.

"Brad can I ask you a question please?" Ben asked, as he was being led through the building to wherever or whatever they had next in store for him. The two were closely followed by Robert Jenkins-Smyth.

"Of course," replied Brad, "you can ask but I may not be able to answer you though."

"Was our hotel room in Washington bugged by the secret service?" Ben asked.

Brad smiled but said "no, of course not, is that why you had the TV on so loud all the time? You were guests of President Carlsen why would we do that."

"Because it's the nature of your job not to trust anybody," Ben replied.

"Don't worry kid, we're all on the same side now," Brad said. "In fact, we've always been on the same side but neither of us knew it then."

Ben followed Brad into a large meeting room which was already occupied by at least 10 military personnel in their smart uniforms. Ben was seated opposite Lizzie who glanced over to him, smiled, and mouthed "are you Ok". Ben smiled back and nodded he was fine. To Ben's right was Robert Jenkins-Smyth and to his left was seated Agent Brad Stringer. Ben also noticed, seated next to Lizzie, was Professor Marie Antony. At the top of the table were two empty seats which were soon taken up by President Carlsen and Michael Grant, the head of the CIA.

Michael Grant stood to address the assembled dignitaries.

"Mr President, ladies and gentlemen, it goes without saying that everything you are about to hear must not leave this room or be electronically transmitted to anyone. I say this really for our British guests who may not be clear on our security protocols. Also, may I just remind you all that no Cell phones or computers are allowed in this room while this meeting is taking place, switched off or not."

Robert Jenkins-Smyth was not impressed with this swipe at the British contingent in the room. *We would not be here if it wasn't for us British,* he thought.

"You have all been made aware," Michael Grant continued, "of how Ben Norton managed to enter this facility and remove a gun, the most valuable asset this facility has acquired in many years. What you are not aware of is that others were also able to enter the base and attempt to steal the gun but failed because Ben had got to it first. They then managed to leave the base without leaving a trace; the base is currently on lockdown as we try to establish who or what it was. Professor Antony, has your team been able to shed any light on this purple smoke that was seen outside the FTD building last night?"

Professor Marie Antony stood to answer.

"No Sir, not yet. We have managed to remove some samples from the exterior of the building, but the smoke or gas is of a composition neither I nor any of my team have ever come across before. My team are still carrying out further tests. We have also concluded, if I may add, that the gun is not of any technology we have come across either. I think the two are linked as it's too much of a coincidence. May I also add that the anti-scanning developed here by my team and coated on all the buildings at Area 51 had kept the gun safe and secure until Ben took it out into the open air."

"I will come back to the gun in a minute," Michael Grant continued. "General Mark, we know how Ben entered the base undetected. Is it possible that others have the same abilities that Ben has? Are we dealing with more invisible threats?"

General Mark stood up to answer.

"As head of military security, at the moment there is no evidence to support the fact others can disappear like Ben, but there is also no evidence to say there are no others that possess Ben's skills. We just don't know. We are still analysing all the security footage of the base and surrounding countryside. But nothing has been found yet. We will of course continue to search." The General then sat down again.

"Ben," Professor Antony asked across the table, "when you saw the purple smoke did you see anything else? What

I'm trying to establish is, when you are invisible, are you able to see others that might be invisible, or have your skill? What I'm getting at, does some terrorist organisation have a similar gun and have worked out how to make other people invisible too?"

All eyes were now on Ben. You could hear a pin drop. The tension in the room was making Ben feel quite uncomfortable. Ben shakily stood up to answer. He was getting quite nervous but thought now was not a good time to disappear.

"No, I have never come across or seen anyone that might possess my skill as you call it. All I have to say about the purple smoke was that it appeared to come from above the ground as if it was being pumped down to the ground, but I didn't stare at it for too long as I took it as an opportunity to escape. I thought it might just be a security device and the gun had been discovered as missing. I don't know what I was thinking apart from getting off the base."

"I would also like to add..." Robert Jenkins-Smyth stood up to speak. "When Ratzilla disappeared in London getting away from my men, some of the locals said they saw a bright light and a purple haze or fog. I can request a team of forensics return to the scene and see if there is any trace and compare that with Professor Antony's samples." Jenkins-Smyth made a quick note to do this as he sat down.

Michael Grant stood up again to continue leading the meeting.

"That would be very useful, Robert," Michael Grant continued. "Everything that is found must be securely relayed to our British counterparts led by Mr. Jenkins-Smyth; in return they will assist us and keep us completely informed. Now with regards the gun, it is the same according to Ben that was used on him by this lunatic calling himself…"

Grant had to double check his notes. "Ratzilla. Is there any news Mr. Jenkins-Smyth on his whereabouts yet?"

Jenkins-Smyth remained seated but just shook his head.

"No, nothing yet" he replied. "We have launched the largest security manhunt in British history, he has simply vanished, excuse the pun."

"Professor Antony and her team have been analysing the gun for over a week now but can't get it to work or understand anything about whom or what made it. Is that correct Marie?" Michael Grant enquired.

"Yes, that is correct sir," Professor Marie Antony replied. Not knowing how something worked or what it was is not something Marie Antony had ever had to deal with before. Let alone twice in one week. She felt defeated for the first time in her life. "But we will keep analysing and testing," Marie added slightly unconvincingly.

"Well, I can disclose to you all that our field operatives have been reporting some very interesting coincidences around the world," Michael Grant continued. "As of yesterday, we have information on 26 countries where there have been robberies where the thief or thieves stunned their victims and made away with cash, gold, diamonds and weapons."

There was a rumble of whispering around the room and people staring at each other, but nobody wanted to be the first to speak.

"Yes, your math is correct, if you have arrived at the total of 28 guns, with the one we have and the missing British one." Michael Grant added. "You will be given a full list of countries straight after this meeting. From this information we must assume that there will be more in the next few days or weeks. It appears the situation is escalating and gathering pace. Twelve of the countries are members of NATO so we must call an emergency meeting ASAP. There is no pattern of either religion, economic or political. We have had our brightest minds looking at all the possible scenarios and they all keep coming back to the same conclusion; We are under attack," Grant hesitated and took a deep breath, "by Extra-terrestrials."

There was stunned silence in the room. Everyone was taking on board what the head of the CIA had just announced.

Ben stared at Lizzie, who was looking at him the same way; they had previously spoken about the gun and its technology not being of this world.

One of the military officers rose to speak when nearly everyone else started speaking at once.

"Please one at a time, you will all get your say," President Carlsen said, raising his voice so he could be heard. "Please carry on, Admiral," President Carlsen said, fighting back his shock at this news.

"Are you saying that the men using the guns, like this Ratzilla person, are really aliens?" Admiral Jones enquired.

"I can answer that for you," Robert Jenkins-Smyth said. "We have traced Ratzilla, his real name is James Ratsby, back to when he was born and beyond. A petty criminal of no note at all, but definitely human. We are still trying to work out why he was chosen. The only solution that makes any sense is that he was easily persuaded to do their bidding, which was to have a nerve gas made by Ben's father, and that's how Ben got involved."

"So, am I right in saying," Admiral Jones continued, "we are being invaded by aliens, yet they give us weapons more advanced than anything we have? It doesn't make sense. Why would they help us?"

"The guns are being given to humans to acquire things they need back home, wherever that is" Michael Grant added. "We don't think the guns can be used against them, but they are not invading either, or we would be constantly under attack."

"The nerve gas that they wanted Professor Norton to make would only kill humans," Robert Jenkins-Smyth interrupted. "What use could that be to them? They gave the formula to the Professor, why not make it themselves? No this is an invasion, and we must act now. We, the British, think that they are trying to disrupt our economies, hence the attempted nerve gas attack on the City of London. I would like to have analysed the locations of the remaining guns and what they wanted the holders to achieve in each location. Are they trying to get us to destroy ourselves, then just waltz onto Earth and take over without any casualties? Are they that clever and advanced?"

Professor Marie Antony stood to speak.

"I think if these aliens, as you want to call them, are so advanced, so intelligent, we must try to make contact with them, not start a war against them. If they can make these guns and are probably involved with the purple gas in some way, we don't know what they are capable of. They may have been on the base yesterday or may be here right now, listening to every word we say."

That started uproar with everyone talking.

Michael Grant tried restoring some order.

"The expert strategists," Grant continued, "believe they are so superior that they don't need to physically fight a war against us, but by stirring things up with the guns and the targets, they have identified our defences would fail. The experts are convinced we are dealing with a very advanced and intelligent species. Their plan appears to be to create a situation where we humans will destroy each other, and they will just use our planet and its resources to create a colony after we wipe ourselves out."

"We must call a special United Nations meeting with all the heads of state immediately," President Carlsen demanded. "We must all pool together everything we each have about these aliens and formulate a plan to start fighting back."

TWENTY-FIVE

Robert Jenkins-Smyth gathered Lizzie and Ben together and informed them that they must return to London as soon as possible.

"You surely now understand how important our next moves are going to be," he said. "For the first time since humans could communicate, we are going to have to trust each other, and more importantly, work together. Or, and I don't say this lightly, it will be the end of the world for all humans."

A furious Professor Antony entered the room where Robert Jenkins-Smyth, Ben and Lizzie were waiting for their helicopter flight to McCarran airport. She was ranting at the top of her voice.

"If it were left to the military, we would all certainly die. Why can't they see that this should be approached in a scientific way? Oh, sorry Robert," she said when she noticed she was not alone. "Do you know what those Generals are suggesting? We stock the underground bunkers and select people to keep the human race alive. Once safely below ground, detonate enough nuclear bombs to decimate the planet. This, they feel, would drive our visitors away. The fact that the planet would be dead for the next two to three hundred years doesn't really matter. Ben, I've been meaning to ask, how is your father? We were at Cambridge together. Giles is one of the cleverest men I know. Please send him my regards will you."

"Yes, certainly," a bemused Ben replied.

Ben and Lizzie were glad to be boarding their flight back to England, and as they were returning with the head of MI6, they were going by private jet.

"Not as nice as Airforce One," Ben said to Lizzie.

"No, we are having to lower our standards," Lizzie replied.

"I'm glad you two are keeping your spirits up," Robert Jenkins-Smyth interrupted. "You have both grown up a lot in the last week. Your country and I are very grateful for everything you have done so far."

"You sound as if our job is over now," Ben said. "I think Lizzie and I have a great deal to offer still."

"It's going to go way above my head now. This is global, and nobody is really prepared for something like this," Robert said, in a very quiet voice, almost whispering. "It will get very messy indeed. America will want to lead, the Russians and China won't let them, and someone will say it's a conspiracy by America to dominate the world. Don't even ask about North Korea. And that's before you even get the religious angle, that we brought it upon ourselves for all these years of promiscuity. Then when it leaks to the media, and it surely will, there will be mass panic on the scale nobody has ever seen before. A real mess, like all your worst nightmares coming true."

"Why has there not been any planning for this sort of thing? There are so many films made about alien invasions, giant meteors and asteroids crashing down to Earth, surely someone thought of putting some sort of contingency plan together?" Ben asked.

"We all have our own plans for invasion or nuclear war, so we will impose that protocol for the British people," Robert replied.

"But what about third world countries that don't have the means or resources? Do we just let them perish?" Lizzie interrupted.

"Hey guys, I'm on your side, but as I have said already, this is way beyond Her Majesty's Government," Robert stated, trying not to raise his voice so the cabin crew could hear. "I'm still hopeful we can contact these creatures and find out what they want, because I agree with Professor Antony; We won't win if it came to war, they appear to be far more advanced than us. Diplomacy has always been the British way, and I think it's the right way on this too."

"Lizzie on our return to London, you are to go to Vauxhall and concentrate on any gun sightings or robberies that could be connected to our visitors, and keep me directly informed," Robert asked. "I will inform your manager that you are on a special assignment and not to be hindered. Ben, you and your father will be moved to a safe house and be protected but must be available at very short notice. It's either that, or you are put under house arrest, and we don't want that do we?"

"Do you think you can contain me if I wanted to leave?" Ben said, very flippantly.

"I will ask your father to assist with the forensics", Robert continued, deliberately avoiding Ben's question, "at the scene of Ratzilla's disappearance and have him liaise with Professor Antony in America."

"Is that all you want from me, to be on standby?" Ben asked, slightly exasperated after all he had done this last week and what had happened to his body.

"Your services will be needed, of that you can be sure Ben," replied Robert. "So please, be patient. We all need to work as a team, especially if America or Russia go in all guns blazing."

"What did President Carlsen want, Ben, when he spoke to you?" asked Jenkins-Smyth, thinking this as good a time as any to ask the question that had been burning in his head since that day in Las Vegas.

"He just told me if there was anything I needed, he would be there for me," Ben replied.

"You are British, and your loyalties are to your Queen and country, Ben, don't forget that" said Jenkins-Smyth.

"I know where my loyalties lie" Ben snapped back, "just don't treat me like a child after what I have been through."

Jenkins-Smyth gave Ben a glare. *You are a very important person at the moment, so I will let that go* he thought to himself, trying to stay calm, as he was not used to people answering him back. *You may even be the key to solving this whole situation.*

Robert Jenkins-Smyth had a car take him back to MI6 whist a chauffeur driven limo took Lizzie to her parents' house, where Lizzie and Ben parted with a long silence and a stare. Their relationship was still friends at the moment, but both felt there should be more. It was very awkward for both of them, but they knew this was not the end of their friendship. Ben, on arriving home, greeted Professor

Norton with a hug so tight he thought he was going to snap his father in half.

"I'm so proud of you Ben," Giles Norton said. "Your mother would be so proud of you saving the American president's daughter from terrorists. How brave is my son."

"Thank you, father," Ben said. "Have you had any luck in coming up with something I can wear that can stick to me when I disappear? Reappearing naked every time caused me so many problems in America and it can be quite embarrassing too."

"No, sorry son, still a work in progress" Professor Norton replied. "If I could get hold of the gun they used on you, I might have a chance. I could create my own source of lightning and test man-made materials as well as natural fibres like silk or cotton. Even make something from a spider's web. Endless possibilities, old chap, just need the gun."

"Professor Marie Antony sends her regards," Ben said. "She says you were at university together. Do you remember her father?"

"Oh yes, Marie Antony," Professor Norton said whilst thinking back to his youth. "A fine young lady if I recall. Your mother didn't like her though. I think your mother was jealous although I never gave her reason to be. I had just started dating your mother when Marie arrived at Cambridge, very confident if I remember rightly. Marie said she was going to get a Nobel Prize for Science before she was thirty, and she did. How is Marie? Working for the President's office the last I heard."

She's fine. Well, sort of. The Americans also have a gun and Professor Antony is the lead scientist trying to work out where it came from and how it works," Ben said. "But she has had no success at all."

"If Marie Antony can't work it out, that would be driving her crazy for sure" Professor Norton interrupted. "Yes, would be the Marie I remember."

"Have MI6 asked you to go back to Maida Vale, Father?" Ben asked.

"Yes," Professor Norton replied. "To help the forensics team. They wouldn't tell me why though. Typical MI6 they have secrets from their secrets. Do you know why, Ben?"

"Of course," Ben said in a very smug way. "When Ratzilla disappeared, some witnesses say they saw some purple-coloured smoke or gas. Well, the night I took the gun out of Area 51, some similar coloured gas or smoke was seen outside the FTD building, which is where Professor Antony was testing the gun. The Americans believe that someone was trying to steal or retrieve the gun, and want to confirm that the smoke was from the same source."

"One moment, young man, go back a bit," Professor Norton interrupted. "You got into Area 51 and stole a gun from under the Americans noses? Area 51?"

"That's correct," Ben said smugly, "with a little help from Lizzie."

"But you're only seventeen! How dare MI6 risk your life like that? You told me you were going on holiday as reward for your help to our government, not some covert mission!" Professor Norton continued.

"MI6 could not have got anywhere near Area 51 without me father," Ben said. "Please calm down and I will fill you in on all the details." Ben spent the next two hours explaining everything to his father including the top-secret meeting with President Carlsen, the head of the CIA Michael Grant, and assorted military personnel.

"If we find any trace of this purple gas, I will insist on taking the samples to America myself," Professor Norton said. "Then team up with Professor Marie Antony. It will be nice to see her again after all these years. I will request that I have a look at this gun, because if we can't solve this puzzle together, nobody on earth can. I really need to find a way to reverse this thing you have, Ben, before it gets you killed for good."

Typical of my father, Ben thought, *has to plan everything down to the last detail. That's why he is a chess grand master. He needs to chill a bit, I might try and get him and Professor Antony together. They obviously like each other. A bottle or two of nice red wine will do them both the world of good.*

As long as there is still a world for them and me to enjoy that is. I'll get Lizzie to help with my matchmaking, Ben said to himself. *Lizzie,* he thought, stopping him in his tracks. *Now that I have met Lizzie it's all going to go wrong, it will be the end of the world. Angus always said I was very unlucky with the girls. Damn it, why is he always so right?*

TWENTY-SIX

It didn't take long for the meeting at the United Nations of all the world's leaders to erupt into a shouting match of conspiracies and accusations. In fact, no fewer than 11 world leaders walked out at various times of the day, returning later to muted applause. But it was only when news of another 12 possible sightings of the guns had been reported that the auditorium became silent, and everyone assembled realised this was really actually happening. The world at large had been told that this emergency meeting was an exercise in case a nuclear war broke out, and they would also discuss world peace and global warming. A ban on all media had been imposed on the premise of security. This would keep a lot of the world's media and troublemakers at bay for long enough for a strategy to be formulated. That was the plan. All the large hotels in New York had been visited by the secret service and were informed if they let any journalist or known troublemakers stay in their hotel, it would be shut down. The one thing everyone was in agreement over was that if the real reason got out before countries were ready, the ensuing panic would be as bad or worse than being taken over by aliens.

A further 24 hours had passed, and they were no closer to an agreement of any kind let alone a solution. In the meantime, a further 5 cases had now been reported, making a total of 45 to date. The aliens obviously knew what the world leaders were up to and had accelerated their plans.

Lizzie was keeping Ben informed about the progress, or lack of progress, in New York.

"It's not looking good, Ben," Lizzie said. "Someone has to take the initiative, or this will be all over, and they will still be in New York blaming each other."

"Have any guns been captured with their operators still alive?" Ben asked.

"Some have, but within 24 hours the guns and holders just disappear," Lizzie replies. "Everyone has reported this purple gas just before the guns vanish, but nobody seems to know what it is or where it comes from."

"So, what is so special about Area 51 that gun was one of the first found and it's still there?" Ben asked. "They did try but I beat them to it. Maybe they don't know its back."

"I find that hard to believe" Lizzie said. "Some of these guns found have been taken from the Russians, the Israelis, and the French. These countries are renowned for the efficiency of their secret services; they don't just lose something like a weapon from outer space. No, Ben, there is something different about Area 51 that we don't know about. Something from it's past. Maybe the crash at Roswell was these same aliens, and they fear Area 51?"

"Maybe Professor Antony was right and the Anti-Scanning stuff they coated on the FTD building was preventing the aliens from tracking the gun." Lizzie stated. "We just don't know for sure."

"Wow, they must be able to travel very fast. I only had the gun outside for a few minutes. Unless…" Ben hesitated for a moment. "Even if they didn't coat the incinerator building, but that would still mean that they got to Area 51 in less than 30 minutes," Ben replied.

"They were not that scared that they tried the night I took the gun" Ben said. Always far more questions than answers.

"Lizzie, I have an idea," Ben said excitedly. "If you want to help me, you need to pack a bag, Lizzie, we are going to America again."

"But Ben, I can't just leave, I'm on a special assignment from Jenkins-Smyth. He'll have my head if I just leave without permission, and he won't give me permission without me explaining why. What crazy idea have you come up with now? I do trust you, Ben, but I need to know more."

"Sorry, Lizzie, of course I will explain to you once we are on our way, but we don't have time now. Please trust me." Ben knew if he told Lizzie his plan to get on board the alien spaceship, assuming they are travelling in a spaceship and not beaming about the planet, she would not go along with him and would try to stop him.

Ben hurried to his father's makeshift study in the safe house. He still knocked before he entered even though it was so important; He could be on the verge of saving the world, the entire planet. Ben asked his father a question he already knew the answer to because Lizzie had informed him earlier.

"When are you going to fly to Las Vegas with the gas samples you have, father?"

"I have a seat booked tonight in about four hours," Professor Norton answered. "Why, Ben, what are you up to?"

"Well, if you and Professor Antony work out how to use the gun, would it not be more sensible if I was close at hand, father?" Ben said.

"Yes, that would be the sensible thing to do. Ok, Ben, go and pack your bag", his father said, "while I get the clearance from MI6." Professor Norton might have appeared to Ben over the years not to be listening, but he knew when his son was scheming, and his son was definitely up to something now. *I'll play along but keep a close eye on him.*

One more thing, father, can you ask Professor Antony if the incinerator building has been covered with their Anti-Scanning stuff, please?"

Ben ran out of the door, then stopped and put his head back into the study. "By the way, father, Lizzie is coming too."

Professor Norton was now completely convinced Ben, and now Lizzie, were up to something.

Ben and his father collected Lizzie from her home and the three of them set off for the airport.

"Did Robert Jenkins-Smyth give you any trouble authorising this trip?" Ben asked.

"No" Lizzie replied. "None at all. He doesn't know. Unpaid leave, I'm calling it. Everyone is far too busy to even notice if I'm in the office or working from home" Lizzie added.

Professor Norton contemplated asking them both outright what they were up to, but he thought better of it; they would only lie anyway. He decided to just keep a very close eye on them instead.

Once they had touched down at McCarran International airport, they were whisked through security to a waiting helicopter which had been arranged by Professor Marie Antony. Soon after, they were greeted by the professor herself outside the FTD building at the centre of Area 51.

"I have arranged for you to stay on the base, Giles. Welcome back Lizzie, Ben." Professor Antony said. "Your message, Ben, was a bit confusing. Are you staying with your father or are you staying with Lizzie in a motel?"

"Can we not stay here on the base?" Ben asked. "I need to be close to my father."

"I will see what I can do," Professor Antony said. "Normally, that would not be possible, but you both already have the highest security clearance, so I will arrange it. But please remember, this is a top-secret base. You can't just wander around. You will be shot. Also, Ben, your father and I are under a lot of pressure to find some solutions to this purple gas, so please no interruptions at all."

"You won't know we are here, I promise," Ben replied.

"Ben, your father says you want to know if the incinerator building is covered with Anti-Scanning paint. No, we felt it was not necessary. Why?" asked Professor Antony.

"It would explain how quickly the aliens arrived to retrieve the gun once I had removed it from the FTD building. If the incinerator building was coated, they would have had only a few seconds to reach the base, but as you say, if it's not coated then they would have had nearly thirty minutes. Far more feasible don't you think?" Ben answered.

"Yes, you could be right, Ben," replied Professor Antony. "They obviously have a tracker of sorts on the guns so they can retrieve them and stop us using their technology against them. Also, it proves my Anti-Scanning coating works, even against these superior beings." the professor continued, smugly.

Professor Norton was escorted by Professor Antony to the lab in the basement where the gun was previously kept, while Ben and Lizzie were taken to their room which was on the third floor of the FTD building: two small beds and a wash basin, in a room smaller than most people's broom cupboards.

"Ok then, Ben, I've waited long enough. What is your master plan for saving the world?" Lizzie demanded. "I have put my career on the line for you. It better be good."

Ben proceeded to explain to Lizzie what he had come up with, and how he was going to save the world. He hoped.

Professor Giles Norton and Professor Marie Antony were now back on first name terms and remembering the better times they had when they were at university back in Cambridge.

"Giles, I hate to say this," Marie said. "These problems of the gun and this gas are beating me. For the first time ever, I feel defeated."

"Let's test the sample I took in London," Giles said, "and compare it to the sample you took here and see if there are any similarities and weaknesses."

"Similarities, there are definitely going to be, of that I'm sure," Marie said. "But finding any weaknesses? We have found none at all. In fact, we have found nothing any of us have seen before. It is not even made of sub atoms, not even subatomic particles. This is not the science we have given our lives to."

"Fascinating, Marie, really fascinating," Giles said. "When was the last time you came across a new branch of science, no, a completely new tree? That's what we have here. We could learn so much from this civilisation."

"Giles, I have been shouting that same tune since all of this came to light a few short weeks ago," Marie stated. "But I am surrounded by warmongers and spies who are all so frightened of their own shadows their only response is to come out all guns blazing. When has mankind had this sort of opportunity before to learn so much in such a short space of time, from intelligence we can only aspire to?"

There was a knock on the security door. Marie looked over and saw Lizzie and Ben outside. They both looked quite frantic and scared. *What's happened now?* Marie thought, as she made her way to let them into the lab.

"The meeting in New York has finished and the news is not great," Lizzie said. "A message is going out to the world looking for anyone that has been given a gun to come forward where they will receive a huge reward. But what isn't being told is that once the gun and user have been handed over to a joint United Nations task force, they will use the gun to lure the aliens somewhere remote and detonate a small nuclear device. This they hope will either be the end of them. or at least it will scare them away."

"And what expert told them that these aliens could be hurt by a nuclear explosion?" Marie asked. "'We can't even see them, they are not made of any chemical composition known to man or anything we recognise, so let's just blow them up, shall we? We are good at destroying things.'"

"A lot of advanced countries are already stock piling and making their deep underground bunkers ready for the fall out and I don't mean nuclear fallout either," Lizzie said.

"Father and Professor Antony I have an idea, but I will need both of you to help me put it in place before these world leaders do something the whole planet will regret," Ben said.

"I knew you were up to something Ben", Professor Norton said.

After going through his plan with Professor Antony and his father, Ben waited for these two eminent scientists to laugh at him and tell him he was mad.

"With the speed that this is all unfolding, we must try everything we can," Professor Antony said. "It's quite a long shot, Ben, but what have we got to lose? Only our reputations, careers, and freedom. We will be locked up, waiting for the end of the world to come. That's exactly what I have spent my whole life working for."

"Marie," Professor Norton said, "If Ben's plan has the remotest chance of success, we must give it a go because the alternatives are all a lot bleaker. I'm prepared to give it a shot and let my son risk his life, and I can assure you Marie, I say that with a very heavy heart."

Ben and Lizzie stared at Professor Antony; it was all down to her, because without her, the plan was a total nonstarter.

"What made you two so confident that you flew all this way knowing that once you told me I wouldn't just stop this in its tracks?" Professor Antony asked.

"Well, I only found out 20 minutes ago," Lizzie said, "but I have faith in Ben. If he thinks it could work, that's good enough for me. We can't just sit back and do nothing."

"For an intelligent lady you have a lot of faith in Ben," Professor Antony stated.

"Normally I don't take uncalculated risks," Professor Antony continued. "I weigh up all the data and make calculated decisions based on fact. I don't know, there is so much at stake here, so much that can go wrong."

"These are not normal times Marie," Professor Norton pleaded, realising she was starting to waver. "These are times where if we don't try everything we can, if we are the lucky ones or not, depending how you view it, we would have to spend the rest of our lives underground. No sun, no seas, and no nature. Is that a life you want?"

"Ok, Ok," Professor Marie Antony declared, "I will help you Ben. Might as well make one crazy and irrational decision in my life before it's all over."

TWENTY-SEVEN

"You don't all need to take this risk," Marie said. "Ben and I can manage on our own. You both should stay on the base."

But Lizzie and Professor Norton would not be deterred from tagging along.

"We're all in this together, Marie," Professor Norton replied. "To the very end. I will not let my son deal with this alone. Well, he eventually will be alone, but I must be there to support him nevertheless."

"My sentiment exactly" Lizzie added.

"I thought you would both say that" Professor Antony said, "so I will arrange security passes off the base for all of us. We are going to Jumbled Hills Pass to carry out some field work, is the official answer if we are asked when leaving the base. You all have high security clearance so we should not have too much trouble. The gun will be hidden under the back seat of my car; I will place some equipment in the trunk to make it look more convincing, which will be searched without fail as we leave the base. You must all be ready in one hour. Now to get the gun out of the lab without causing suspicion." Professors Antony and Norton made their way down to the basement lab in the FTD building where numerous colleagues of Professor Antony were busy on several experiments, trying to break down the chemical composition of the purple gas.

Professor Antony followed by Professor Norton went over to the bench where two of her assistants were trying to take samples of the gun metal but were having no luck.

"Ah, Professor, you are back," a slim young man said as the two professors approached. "This metal is indestructible; I cannot even get the smallest sample to analyse. We have heated it and frozen it and applied enormous amounts of pressure, but the structure does not alter at all. It's amazing whatever it is."

"Thank you, Frederick," Professor Antony said. "Professor Norton and I will take over from here."

"Yes, certainly" the young scientist replied, as he and his colleague left the lab bench and proceeded to join another group at the far end of the lab.

"Since the gun was returned, security has been stepped up even more, if that's possible" Professor Antony stated. "The gun has had a tracker fitted by the CIA and only they can remove it."

"Do you have any idea how we can remove the tracker from the gun, then get it out of the lab and give us enough time to leave the base?" Professor Norton asked. "Or do you trust all your team to cover for us?"

"I trust my team explicitly, but I don't want to put them in a position where they are all putting their careers on the line too," Professor Antony said. "If Ben's plan does not work, we will all be arrested for treason. Therefore we must remove the gun without anyone noticing. I have an idea on how to remove the tracker. I will ask permission for the tracker to be removed whilst we attempt a very extreme heat experiment on the gun. My head is going to be on the block anyway whatever the outcome, so it doesn't matter. After all, how many times can they execute me for treason?"

"Why do we need to remove the tracker if we are going to place the gun in a box coated with your Anti-Scanning paint?" We know it works really well," asked Giles Norton.

"Because once we remove the gun from the box so the aliens can track it, the CIA will also be made aware it is off the base and come looking for it," answered Marie Antony.

"Once the tracker is removed, we can tell my team we are heading to the incinerator to carry out the tests," Professor Antony continued. "That should buy us enough time to get off the base and place our trust, and lives, and careers in Ben's hands."

"Ben won't let us down," Professor Norton said. "I will be with you all the way, and if you go down, I'm going down with you."

"Thank you for your support, Giles," Professor Antony replied. "Let's just make sure we give Ben every opportunity to succeed. Not only for us, but all of mankind."

Professor Antony made the call to the CIA about the removal of the tracker, but the CIA were insistent that a team of agents remain with the gun the whole time the tracker was removed.

"Our plan hasn't even started, and we have been stopped at the very first hurdle," Professor Antony said, whilst trying to see what Professor Norton was doing huddled over the gun.

"Call the CIA back and tell them we have changed our plans and you don't need them to remove the tracker," Professor Norton said.

"But why, Giles? We can't proceed with the tracker still on or all hell will break loose once we remove it from the coated box," Professor Antony stated.

"No need to worry about the tracker," Professor Norton said, turning towards Professor Antony holding the tracker in his hand. "It just fell off in my hand."

"How did you manage to remove it Giles?" Professor Antony asked.

"I read a paper about this exact technology last year. It's British you know. Quite simple if you know what you are doing," Professor Norton said. "Marie, lock the tracker in your office for safe keeping whilst I put the gun in the box. Then we can meet Ben and Lizzie."

"Well, this is the point of no return. If anyone wishes to bail out, now is your chance," Professor Antony said as they assembled by her car outside the FTD building. "No takers? Then let's go and save the world. Literally."

The car with the four on board approached the double security checkpoint at the perimeter fence. There was a queue of about six vehicles all being meticulously checked before they were allowed to leave the base. The ten minutes it took waiting made the tension in the car even greater than it was before. They stopped once they got to the front of the queue and all had to exit the vehicle, which was quite normal but very nerve-racking, nevertheless. The trunk was opened and was being checked. Even though Professor Antony was a very senior scientist, security was so tight even the President's car would be checked over.

"Please be careful, that's all very delicate equipment." Professor Antony said to one of the guards checking over the vehicle. Ben stood watching nervously, unable to help as the car was searched, hoping that the guards would not check under the back seat of the car. Ben was by now very skilled at not getting nervous. Lizzie was getting better too after the last couple of weeks with Ben, but both the Professors were starting to sweat a bit more. This was not normal for them at all.

After a couple of minutes, they were allowed to re-enter their car and drive through to the next checkpoint, ten yards away. *That was close,* they all thought, trying not to look too suspicious. At the second checkpoint they handed the guard all the security documents. He then keyed in their details one by one. The guard looked up and stared at Professor Antony. *Something was wrong*, they all thought.

"Keep calm," Professor Norton whispered, "just keep calm." The guard left his cubicle and slowly walked over to the vehicle holding the documents in his hand. He bent down at the driver's door.

"You must return to the base immediately, Professor Antony."

"Why?" demanded the professor.

"I'm sorry, Professor Antony," said the guard, "but there is an order here which states that you and Professor Norton are not to leave the base under any circumstances."

"By who's authority?" demanded Professor Antony.

"By the President himself, ma'am" replied the guard.

"I'm sorry but you will all have to return to the base immediately."

"Professor Antony," Lizzie interrupted, "Ben and I can carry out the tests on our own, we know what to do."

"Yes," Ben added. "We will be fine, and time is running out."

Professor Norton placed his left hand on Professor Antony's shoulder, squeezed it slightly and said:

"They will be fine Marie. They can do it."

Professor Antony reluctantly told the guard that she and Professor Norton would return to the FTD building on foot and Lizzie would carry on with the field experiment with Ben as her assistant.

As Lizzie drove the car off the base, she could see in her rear-view mirror both Professors Norton and Antony standing like parents who were watching their children leave for university for the first time, hoping the children could cope by themselves and feeling helpless at the same time.

Lizzie turned right and headed towards Jumble Hills Pass. It didn't take long for them to arrive at a secluded spot, perfect for what they had planned. It was early evening now and the sun was setting in the distance, great if they had planned a picnic but they were here for a far more important reason.

"Ok, Lizzie," Ben said, "take the gun out of the box and place it on that little mound, then drive the car down to that curve in the road and park up. You must stay in the car with the doors locked at all times. I will be fine as long as you are safe. Remember, they can't hurt me."

Lizzie leant over to Ben and gave him a kiss on the cheek.

"You don't know what they can do, Ben. You are not invincible," Lizzie said, fighting back a tear. "Just remember that, keep safe and come back please. I will be waiting for you."

Ben smiled at Lizzie, wiped the tear from her face, then he vanished, leaving a pile of clothes on the seat next to her. Lizzie took the box containing the gun from under the rear seat, removed the gun, and placed it on the mound as instructed. She then drove the car to the bend in the road and waited. If Ben was right that they must have tracking devices of some sort within the laser guns, the aliens should be coming soon. Very soon. If not, then they would just keep on waiting until it was dark, then return to the base with the bad news.

Ben remained invisible at a spot near the base of the mound where he could keep an eye on the gun, but he could not see Lizzie clearly, so he decided to go over to the car and wait there but remain invisible. He was floating next to Lizzie who had gotten out of the car to stretch her legs, both looking out into the distant sky for something to happen. The tension was enormous but the importance of getting it right was even greater.

That's when Ben first saw the craft. It was approaching them at a rapid speed. This made his pulse race even faster. Ben turned to look at Lizzie, but she was still just gazing into the sky. *That's it*, Ben thought. *She can't see the spacecraft, only I can because I'm invisible. I was right and my plan may just work. They have the ability to be invisible too. This means they probably can see me if they have eyes. Maybe they have other senses and don't have eyes or hands.* His mind was racing in every direction.

Ben was getting excited at what was about to happen and the importance of the mission. He would have to be very careful; Ben hadn't planned on them being able to see him. In fact, his plan had a great deal of faults, but three very intelligent people had gone along with this scheme. Were they all so desperate for Ben to succeed that nobody had questioned his plan with any great detail, not even his father?

As the spacecraft drew nearer, Ben thought *that's not what I thought it would look like, it's not aerodynamic but it appears to be made of the same shiny alloy as the gun*, although he really only thought that it would not look like a flying saucer, apart from that he had no idea. It was not that large, about the size of a detached house. Ben could not see any jet engine or any other form of propulsion, but this thing moved in on them at a great speed, nevertheless. Ben's mind was racing with what these creatures looked like, how did they communicate, and more importantly would they listen to him or just kill him? They were not here peacefully, Ben knew that much, otherwise they would not be distributing these guns all over the world.

"What was I thinking?" Ben said to himself, now having second thoughts. "They won't listen to me." Thankfully, Lizzie had now got back into the car and locked the door. Ben took a deep breath and hurried over to where the gun was. He knew he would have to be quick. Ben would only have one chance, so he couldn't afford to get it wrong. There is no going back now. Ben turned to look at Lizzie, hoping it wasn't the final time he would see this beautiful brave young lady.

As the spacecraft hovered ten feet above the gun, a

purple mist or smoke was sprayed from beneath the craft. Ben noticed Lizzie now staring at the smoke. She was beautiful, he thought. Ben struggled to see, but just made out what appeared to be a small trap door opening and a metal cylinder being lowered, covering the gun. *I must move now,* Ben thought. His pulse was racing so fast and loud, if they couldn't see him, they surely could hear him.

Ben floated up and into the spacecraft.

TWENTY-EIGHT

So, this is what an alien spaceship looks like, Ben thought, as he scanned the darkness around him. *Very dark inside, no windows or lights. I didn't think I would see an Edison light bulb but some sort of light. Are they nocturnal?* Ben thought, *or are they blind? Maybe they really don't have eyes.* Ben reached out with his arms outstretched to feel his way forward. The walls felt cold like they were made of cold steel, but he knew they were probably the same as the guns. After a few minutes, he got used to the gloom and could make out a larger area ahead. Ben was trying to be very quiet, but his heart was beating ten to the dozen and pounding his chest so hard he thought it would push through his rib cage. It also dawned on him, as he walked on the cold metal floor, he was totally naked and vulnerable. Not the way he wanted to meet these creatures, or his maker, for that matter, whichever turned out to be his destiny. Ben edged forward slowly.

Still no sign of any life. Everything was made of this shiny alloy, as he entered the larger domed area. Ben noticed, through the gloom, the cylinder that had been lowered to suck up the gun. *Ok,* he thought, *this must be some sort of loading bay.* There were a number of round containers covering about half the far wall. Ben gingerly made his way across the dome towards these containers, not knowing what he would find inside them. The first one, about three feet in diameter, was full of guns. *So, they are going round the world retrieving their guns. After a quick and rough count,* Ben thought, *there are about fifty here, which hopefully means this is the only alien craft targeting Earth.* Ben was thrilled there was only one crew of aliens to persuade to leave them alone, not a fleet of them. The container next to that one was full of clothes: human looking clothes. *So, they are like us,* he thought, *not some monster with a huge head, but the same size and shape as humans. Or were they humans that could travel back in time? If they were time travellers, why are they trying to destroy themselves? This is even more confusing,* as a million different ideas were swirling round and round in his head.

Ben reached down into the container and started looking through the clothes for things that might fit him. *I don't think they will mind if I borrow some clothes and get dressed.* He selected a pair of jeans, a white T-shirt, and some trainers, noticing they all had labels like the clothes we have on earth, but in a foreign language. *Really strange,* he thought, and then he remembered he was on an alien spaceship, rummaging through their recycled clothes container. The third and final container had plants, flowers, fruit, and vegetables in, all just piled on top of each other. *They will get food poisoning if this is how they store their food,* Ben said, shaking his head whilst tutting. *You're not that bright after all,* he thought, *you have no food hygiene skills at all.*

I need to make some sort of contact now before they fly off. I hope they speak English; my Latin and French are really poor. Father always said learning another language would come in useful, I don't think he had this sort of situation in mind though when he was telling me to study hard. Active revision was his answer to any test or exam. Active revision he would repeat time after time. Ben would go to bed with those words ringing in his ears; "active revision is the only way to be successful in your exams."

Ben entered another curved corridor which he hoped would lead to their control room. He had been on board now for nearly ten minutes and no alarm had gone off. Did they know he was on board but were not frightened? If they *had* that sort of emotion. He did start to feel a little safer and was now having to make himself stay invisible (*this is getting so confusing, I need to keep concentrating before it all goes wrong*) by keeping his pulse rate high, because if he became visible on the ship he would probably fall out of the spacecraft and the opportunity of communicating with them would be lost. *Maybe they are not out to destroy the world,* he tried to convince himself, and then he remembered the nerve gas they wanted his father to make. This was going to be set off around the City of London, the centre of the world's business community, which would cause financial meltdown across the world. *No, Ben, keep focused. These things are not your friends* he had to say to himself whilst keeping his pulse racing.

Ben entered the next dome shaped chamber; this one was larger than the previous one and had a large number of rectangular shaped containers in. Ben made his way to the nearest container and slowly leaned over and looked inside.

He jumped back with shock at what he saw inside. It had the naked body of a man inside. *Is he asleep?* Ben wondered. *Should I wake him up? He looks human,* he thought. Ben took a deep breath and went back over to the container.

Leaning over he gently lowered his trembling hand very slowly until he touched the cold skin of what appeared to be a dead body. Ben checked for any vital signs of life but there were none. *If he's an alien, is this how they travel about, in a coma like state? But there is no pulse,* he reminded himself. *Maybe they don't have hearts like we do, and he is just sleeping?* Ben thought.

Ben moved onto the next container, but it was the same again, another naked man. He moved from one to the next until he came across a body he recognised.

"So, that's what happened to you," Ben said out loud, as he stood over the body of Ratzilla. "Wake up and smell the coffee" Ben said to himself. *The guns they have recaptured are out there in the other chamber and these are the bodies of the men they entrusted to carry out their bidding. They are tidying up after themselves. So, I'm wearing a dead man's clothes,* Ben shuddered with the thought. *Not very nice people are they, not nice at all, these aliens. On reflection, all the bodies here were of men who were out to line their own pockets at the expense of mankind, so I shouldn't feel too sorry for them. I wonder what they are going to do with them. Are they going to try and recreate man on their planet, is that why they have the food and vegetation?*

Ben quickly ran round and checked all the containers. Some were empty but all the full containers had one thing in common. He stopped and smiled. *They are going to have a job recreating humans with this lot; they are all men!* He laughed, but had to be very careful to keep his heartbeat racing. Ben couldn't stop seeing the funny side to this though. These things, creatures or whatever they are, are so intelligent, so advanced, but they don't know about the birds and the bees! This made him laugh even more. He was finding it very hard now not to let his pulse slow down. Ben decided to go back to Ratzilla's container to say a final goodbye to the man that had changed Ben's life forever.

On peering into the container Ben noticed a slightly raised section of metal about two centimetres square near the top lip of the container. Without thinking, he just touched it gently, out of curiosity as you do. Suddenly, the container started to vibrate quite violently. Startled, Ben took a couple of steps back.

"Oh no, what have I done now!" he said to himself. "If they did not know I was on board before they certainly do now." After a couple of seconds, the vibrating stopped, so Ben decided to see what he had started. He gingerly crept forward and peered into the container. As he did so, a hand came up and grabbed him by the throat, trying to pull him into the container. Ben was fighting with all his strength to stay out of the container and break free from whatever it was that had got hold of his throat and was now choking him. With a show of strength from a truly desperate man, Ben managed to break free from this vice-like grip and pull away. He did not need to try and keep his pulse racing; it was pounding like never before. What had he done and what was it that was trying to strangle him? Ben did not have to wait long to get the answers to his questions. Something was now rising from the container. *What do I do? Run,* he thought, *but where? I'm on an alien spaceship and I have just woken up the enemy.*

"You. It had to be you." said the voice, as the figure emerged from the container.

Ratzilla was now standing up in the container and peering through the gloom at Ben.

"Well, you could say thank you for waking you up and trying to save you instead of trying to strangle me," Ben replied, pleased with himself for coming up with that excuse so quickly.

"Waking me up? What do you mean waking me up and trying to save me?!" Ratzilla demanded. Then, looking down, realised he was naked and dropped down a little to cover his modesty. "Where am I, why am I naked, how did you get here, what the hell is going on?"

"Slow down, slow down," Ben said, trying to calm Ratzilla down. "Don't you know where you are? Have you not had contact with the aliens yet?"

"Aliens?" Ratzilla bellowed at Ben, "Have you gone mad, or have you just bumped your head heavily? Very heavily."

"We are on board an alien spaceship," Ben replied. "The same aliens that sent you the gun and wanted you to make the nerve gas to destroy London."

"I don't understand," Ratzilla said. "Everything is very fuzzy and confusing. Was it you that brought the police or whoever to my place? I remember a shootout and me escaping through the sewers, but nothing else until now."

"It appears you were captured and brought on board their ship once your part of the deal had gone wrong," Ben said. "It also appears they have decided to change their invasion of Earth by not using humans. This craft is tidying up and is getting ready to leave, I think, but it looks like they are taking some souvenirs home with them. You were one of their souvenirs. Just look in all the containers: others like you sent a gun and given a mission to complete. I think they have cancelled this attack for now, but they will probably be back."

"So, what are you doing here?" Ratzilla asked, still trying to come to terms with everything Ben had just told him.

"I'm on a mission" Ben answered, "to try and persuade these things that we are a peaceful race, and we can help each other. We can learn so much from them, they are so much more advanced than us, but I'm sure given the chance we can teach them things too. We might be able to help them find whatever it is that they are seeking."

"I think they are just trying to expand their empire," Ratzilla replied. "You're on a mission for who? Why would the authorities send a kid?"

"Because thanks to you shooting me and being hit by lightning at the same time, I can make myself invisible and fly, which is how I managed to escape from you and get on board this ship, which is currently floating over the Nevada desert."

"Nevada U.S.A.?" barked Ratzilla.

"Yes" Ben quickly replied, "you have probably been around the world dozens of times since you were captured."

"So, what is your plan now that you are on board?" Ratzilla asked, his voice sounding very shaky.

"Well, I don't have a plan as such," Ben replied. "My mission is to tell them we want to talk not fight, before a Third World War starts. There are clothes in a container down that corridor," he said, pointing to the way he had entered this chamber. "Get dressed I may need your help."

Ben was hoping he could trust Ratzilla now he was aware of what he had helped to create and what this could all lead to if they failed.

Ratzilla hesitated for a moment then climbed out of the container, covering himself up with his hands, and walked towards where Ben was pointing. Ratzilla returned a few minutes later wearing his own clothes which he managed to find in the container.

"That's better" Ratzilla said, "it's amazing how vulnerable you feel without clothes on, even in this situation."

"Ok, follow me" Ben demanded, as if to say *I'm the boss now*. "We need to find their control room."

From this chamber there was another passageway. Ben didn't know whether he was walking to the front or the rear of the spacecraft. Ratzilla just quietly followed. Ben had completely lost his bearings, but he would have to carry on. Slowly he made his way down the metal corridor and again it led to a dome shaped space, but this one was different; apart from being completely empty, it gave him a very eerie feeling that they were being watched . There were no other tunnels or corridors. He had come to the end of the road as far as he was concerned.

"Well, what now?" Ratzilla asked .

Ben, on not discovering any physical aliens or some sort of control room, was at a total loss of what to do next.

Out of sheer frustration, he just shouted out as loud as he could.

"We are here in peace! We mean you no harm!" Ben paused as if waiting for a reply he could understand. But nothing happened. "Tell us what you want or need from our planet, we could help you!" he shouted, his voice becoming more desperate. "We want to help you!" he continued. But still nothing. "We are a peaceful race of humans who won't hurt you or your kind, we can learn so much from each other!" Ben waited again, hoping for something, anything, but still there was nothing. Ben turned and looked in total despair at Ratzilla, who was looking equally bemused.

"Where are you then?" Ben continued to shout. "We are here and not afraid of you!" he said, trembling, and not being very convincing. "Show yourselves you cowards, what do you want from us? I know you can understand me, you sent out instructions to Ratzilla in English." Then suddenly Ben stopped shouting, as if he was convinced they would answer him.

Ratzilla was getting less and less sure that Ben knew what he was doing, but could not come up with any solutions or alternatives himself.

Ben smiled, then turned, whispering to Ratzilla: "My father always said the best way to deal with bullies is with humour."

"Ok then, Ben," Ratzilla said, sarcastically, "tell them a joke, they may unload us all, say sorry, and leave."

"Two lions walking down Oxford Street in the middle of the day, one turned to the other and said, 'I thought you said it was busy here'" Ben said, smiling.

"Is that the best you can do?" Ratzilla asked. "I remember when I was a young boy there was a television advert for mashed potatoes and the aliens were watching humans making mashed potatoes the proper way, with real potatoes. and killing themselves laughing. Keep it up, Ben, it might work."

"I split up with my cross-eyed girlfriend today" Ben said. "I think she is seeing someone else."

This did not even get a smile from Ratzilla.

"What did Sushi A say to Sushi B? Wasabi," Ben continued.

"Some cannibals were eating a comedian, one turned to the others and said, does this taste funny to you?"

"Really?" Ratzilla said, "This is the best our government can come up with? Get on board an invading spaceship and tell them the worst jokes in the world? We should just let them have Earth if that's the best we can do!"

Then suddenly the room lit up with this bright white light that seemed to come up from the floor. They then heard a voice just like Ben's, in fact it *was* Ben's voice that spoke out.

"Your planet Earth is dying; you are killing yourselves, there is nothing here for us now."

"What did you want with Earth?" Ben asked. But there was no reply.

"Where are you from?" Ben asked. Again, there was no reply.

"We mean you no harm!" Ben shouted, getting more and more frustrated with the silence.

Just then, Ben and Ratzilla felt a thrust of power from below as if the spacecraft was flying upwards at great speed.

"I think it's time to leave" Ben said to Ratzilla. But how? Ben turned and ran as fast as he could back down the corridor. "Quick, follow me!" he shouted to Ratzilla. "You see, my jokes worked after all" he said, pleased with himself.

Ratzilla just shook his head and followed Ben.

They went past all the dead or frozen bodies and into the chamber where the guns were. *Think, Ben, quick, think.* The spaceship was still powering up, time was running out.

Ben went over to the metal cylinder in the middle of the chamber.

"What if we try sliding down that chute, there might be a trap door we could open and jump out?" Ben tried to float up to the top of the cylinder, but he was firmly stuck to the ground. *I can't fly, why have my powers deserted me now when I need them most?*

"Of course!" he said out loud, "everything on this ship is invisible, it's the reverse of what's on the ground!"

"I will go back and talk to the aliens, I will try and reason with them, maybe they will land and let us go, or at least I will buy you some more time, Ben," Ratzilla said. "I don't have a parachute, and unlike you, Ben, I can't fly. You must escape and let the world know what has happened here. If everything here is the reverse, you need to become visible surely to get off the ship."

"But I can't just leave you here" Ben replied.

"Yes, you can, in fact, you must. I don't know, maybe my adventure is about to start" Ratzilla said. "My life can't be any worse than it was back on Earth. You go young man, you have your whole life ahead of you (but not as a comedian). Just go now! Ben, please let them know I was not all bad." With that Ratzilla turned and ran towards the empty chamber with such a spring in his step as if he had finally found his calling in life.

"Ok, Ben, calm down, you need to slow you heart rate down," He started to take deep breaths. *This is not easy* he thought to himself, *I'm being flown at speed away from Earth and towards their planet and the only way I can survive is to calm down. If I survive this, I'm going to learn yoga I promise. What about meditation?* Ben thought, *Let's give it all a try!* as he sat down on the cold metal floor. *Ok* he thought *you sit down and cross your legs like this, then you put your arms out and close your eyes I think you chant something, but I don't know what. Take deep breaths, Ben, in through the nose, out through the mouth, or is it the other way round? Never mind, just do one or the other,* he said out loud. *Breathe in, hold, breathe out, breathe in, hold, breathe out.*

Suddenly Ben felt cold air around him and a sinking feeling; he opened his eyes slowly to see. He was plummeting down to earth at a very fast speed indeed and still in his sitting position. *Where was the spaceship?* He looked up but there was nothing. It was gone. Ben made his pulse race faster, which isn't very difficult when you are falling down to earth at two hundred miles an hour without a parachute. Ben vanished again, then looked up. The spaceship was gone. *Was it like a drone being driven from their home planet? Of course!* Ben thought, *why would they spend years travelling when they can control everything from their own base? Wow, they must be super intelligent creatures.*

"Good luck, Ratzilla" he heard himself say out loud. His momentum was still taking him down to earth but he could now control this and slow himself down to have a safer landing. As the ground below grew nearer, he tried to identify where he was, look for something familiar.

TWENTY-NINE

Ben landed on the edge of a very built-up area with many modern high-rise buildings. *What part of the USA am I in?* he thought. It was quite an affluent city for sure, but not one he had seen before. Looking round for a clue, he froze when he read the sign a couple hundred feet in front of him. Singapore Zoo, the large white and green sign read.

"Singapore!" he said out loud. He was calm and visible. How fast was that spaceship travelling? He quickly put his hands down to cover his modesty as there were a lot of people about, but surprisingly nobody was paying him any notice. Ben looked down and saw he was still wearing the white T-shirt, jeans, and trainers. *I must still be invisible he thought*. But before he could do anything about it, someone bumped into him.

"Sorry" they said to him in an English accent, and carried on walking. *What just happened?* Ben thought. *This can't be right. These clothes are from the spaceship,* he thought, *they must do something to them or they would be visible when the ship is flying. At least now I won't have to run around naked every time I reappear. I need to phone the base and get in touch with father and Professor Antony. I'll stop a policeman if I have too. This is too important to just wait.*

"Lizzie!" Ben shouted out loud, then a lot of people turned and stared at him. *Lizzie might still be waiting by the car. How long have I been gone? Thirty minutes?* he thought. *Surely no more than an hour? Wow,* Ben thought, *that spaceship did Las Vegas Nevada to Singapore in less than an hour, when I get home, I'm going to work that out exactly, must be at least seven or eight thousand miles an hour or more.*

After walking around for a while not seeing a policeman or police car, he decided to go into the first shop he saw and ask them for help. Eventually, the shop keeper did call the police, and once back at the station, he was allowed to call the police in London who put him through to MI6.

"What the hell are you doing Ben?!" shouted Robert Jenkins-Smyth down the phone. "Ringing from Singapore, you did say Singapore, at four in the morning?! Why are you not with your father at Area 51, and how did you get to Singapore?" Robert Jenkins-Smyth stopped himself, and even in his sleepy state, realised they were talking on an open phone line.

"The alien spaceship…" Ben started to answer.

"Stop, don't say another word," Jenkins-Smyth interrupted. "This line is not secure. You will have plenty of time to explain when you get back to Area 51. I will be making my own way there myself. It better be good, Ben, or you and your father are in big trouble."

The British consulate for Singapore himself came and collected Ben, then drove him straight to Singapore Changi airport. But before he boarded his flight, he was allowed to call the base and speak with his father.

"Don't worry, Ben," Professor Norton said. "I will get Marie to send a car to collect Lizzie. Did you manage to speak to our guests while you were away?"

"Yes, father," Ben replied, "but I don't know if it went well or not."

"At least you tried, son, and you are safe now," Professor Norton said.

The flight back to Las Vegas via Los Angeles, then a helicopter ride to the base, was a lot longer, Ben thought, *than the outbound flight on the spaceship.*

Lizzie was waiting for Ben at the base accompanied by Professor Antony and Ben's father, Giles. Lizzie was definitely the happiest to see him. She even did that thing you see in films and ran in slow motion with outstretched arms into his embrace.

"I'm so glad you're safe, Ben," Lizzie said. "One minute the gun was there, and then it got covered in that purple smoke. When the smoke disappeared, the gun had gone too. When you didn't reappear again, I didn't know if you got on board the spaceship, or if they captured you. I called your name out over and over again, and then I just waited. When the car came to pick me up, I thought you were dead, really dead, for good," she said, wiping a solitary tear from her eye.

"Glad to see you are safe, Ben," Professor Antony said in a very matter of fact way. "We should save the reminiscing for inside my office where it's more private. Then, checking to see if Ben had any luggage, she asked where the gun was.

"They have it back," Ben replied.

Once back in Professor Antony's office, Ben started to describe what had happened to him on board the alien spaceship, the finding of the dead or frozen bodies including Ratzilla's and the part Ratzilla played in his escape, the food, and the clothes. Ben carefully explained the conversation he had had with the alien, and how he managed to set himself free with his version of yoga meditation.

Professor Antony asked Ben to repeat the conversation he had with the alien another two times, each time asking:

"Was he sure that is exactly what was said word for word?"

"Yes, definitely," Ben stated. "I might not have the memory recall that Lizzie has, but that conversation will stay with me forever. The exact words were "Your planet Earth is dying; you are killing yourselves, there is nothing here for us now.""

"Then they flew up into space?" Lizzie asked Ben. "Do you think they were heading home? Wherever that is."

"Yes, I do" Ben replied, "I think it's all over."

"I hope your right, Ben," Professor Antony said. "We still have to explain to the president why we smuggled the gun out of the base and have now lost it or given it back."

"Surely it was worth the risk if our actions have saved the whole planet" Lizzie remarked.

"Yes, maybe," Professor Antony replied. "But we still committed treason by stealing something that belonged to the United States Government. The end does not always justify the means. We shall have to deal with any fallout that comes our way. The most important thing now is to inform both our governments what happened and hope there are no more sightings of guns or purple smoke."

"I don't want to spoil the party," Lizzie said, "but do you think the aliens might come back if they realise they only have male versions of our species and need a female to reproduce?"

"That will only be answered in time," Professor Antony said. "It sounds like this Ratzilla chap tried to come good in the end after all."

Meanwhile, the whole time Ben was telling the story of his adventure in an alien spacecraft, his father was staring and touching Ben's t-shirt and jeans.

"Amazing, they can make any human fibre go invisible when you are invisible, and reappear when you reappear," Professor Norton said. "Absolutely amazing technology. I need to run some tests, Ben, on your clothes and shoes. Don't wash them, just bag them up for me."

"Sorry, Dad, but I need these clothes" Ben said. "Do you know how embarrassing it is every time you vanish your clothes just fall off? Then the first thing you must do on reappearing is find something to wear? Not always that easy."

"Ok, son, I understand," Professor Norton said. "Next time you have a few hours to spare I would like to look at their molecular structure to see how it has been changed, that's all. I will let you have them back in one piece."

Five days had now passed since the four got an almighty dressing down from Michael Grant, the head of the CIA, and his MI6 counterpart Robert Jenkins-Smyth. Lizzie had been ordered to return to London, whilst Professors Antony and Norton were still analysing Ben's clothes and the purple gas. Ben had reluctantly allowed himself to be analysed by a large team of British and American scientists to see what makes him disappear and reappear. Also, to make sure he hadn't brought any alien germs or bugs back with him from his trip on the spacecraft.

The official line to the other world leaders is to wait and prepare to go underground. The Russians and the Chinese were sure the British and Americans were hiding something, but did not know what. They were though all thankful for the extra time to get ready and protect as many of their people as they could.

"It's been 12 days, Lizzie," Ben said during one of their daily phone calls, "since I last saw you, and 14 since my little chat with you know who over Singapore. When do you think things will get back to normal?"

"I don't know, Ben," Lizzie said. "But every day that passes the tension here in Vauxhall gets less and less. There is another reason why I rang you, Ben. You are going to be speaking to the United Nations on Sunday to all the world leaders."

"Firstly, why me?" Ben replied, "And secondly, how come you knew before me?"

"You forget where I work, Ben," Lizzie said. "Anyway, someone has to watch out for you. You've already proven you are hopeless on your own. Why you? Well, you did save the planet, so it has to come from you. I will write a speech for you if you like. I know what you are like with public speaking. I will make you look good, don't worry."

"You can be as righteous as you want, Lizzie, but you forget who's the hero around here: it's me."

Lizzie was laughing at Ben.

"Righteous, really? I don't think you can use that word in that context" Lizzie said. "I will definitely have to write your speech for you."

"You knew what I meant, young lady," Ben replied. He could feel the heat of Lizzies burning anger at being called young lady. That was her Achilles heel; he also knew he would pay for that dearly when they next meet.

"I don't know why I bother looking out for you," Lizzie said. "Insulting me like that. When are the scientists planning on releasing you so you can come home, Ben?"

"Never, if the scientists have their way," Ben replied. "I've told my father that I will give them another four weeks and then I'm off, but he is so engrossed in his work with Professor Antony. I don't get to see him very much."

"Do you think, Ben," Lizzie asked, "there could be anything going on with your father and Professor Antony? I mean romantically."

"I'm not sure," Ben said. "Maybe in time, they currently spend every waking moment together working in the lab. A romantic evening for them is a takeaway pizza looking through a microscope and doing endless tests. I do like Marie, though, that's what she wants me to call her. I haven't seen my father this happy in years. Do you think they will want me to disappear in front of the United Nations on Sunday? Because I'm not a performing monkey." Ben said, dramatically changing the subject.

"I don't know, Ben," Lizzie said. "But I will find out what your speech should contain and how much information you will be allowed to divulge regarding your skills."

"Will it just be a speech, or will it be followed by questions? Ben asked.

"I don't know," Lizzie said. "You will be briefed beforehand and probably have an earpiece so you can be guided with your answers during the address. If it gets out you have the ability to disappear and reappear, your life will be ruined. Every country will want to carry out tests on you and you would also be at risk of kidnap the rest of your life."

"Oh great," Ben said. "I will be put on display to the world to see and then have to lie about what I did for the world."

"Well, not lie exactly" Lizzie said. "We will have to change a few things on how you got on board and escaped. The rest of the details can be the same."

"I have an idea," Ben said. "I would say I was taken like all the others because I had a gun too, onto the spaceship but managed to escape after persuading them to leave Earth alone."

There was a small pause while Lizzie thought about Ben's plan.

"That sounds more farfetched than the truth" Lizzie said. "If you start spinning lies you will be found out. You have had better plans before, Ben."

"So, I will refuse to address the United Nations" Ben said. I don't see how putting me out on display will achieve anything."

"There is great tension at the moment between quite a few countries, and distrust," Lizzie stated. "The rumours are that there were no aliens and that it was all a plan by one of the superpowers to take ultimate control of the world. The Americans and British are getting the blame because we seemed to be calm and take control after you returned from Singapore. World War Three could be started after this. We get rid of an alien threat then we just blow ourselves up because we don't trust each other?"

"I have another plan," Ben shouted out excitedly. "Are you sure this line is ultra-safe Lizzie?"

"Yes, very safe," Lizzie replied. "The line between MI6 and Area 51 is encrypted and on a very secure line."

"Listen to this; I could address the United Nations as one of the aliens. All I would need is a costume that would cover my face and body and distort my voice. Then when I finished telling the assembled world leaders that we the aliens would leave their planet alone, I would then disappear. They would believe that, and everything would go back to normal."

"You may have something there, Ben," Lizzie said. "You may have found a solution that could work. As long as the world's leaders don't think it's a trick, it could just work. The costume could be a protective suit like the ones engineers use on radioactive sites a full body and head suit. The statement could read the suit is to stop the alien from catching human diseases and protect Earth from alien infections."

It was Sunday evening and the world's leaders were assembled for what they had been told was the greatest day since man had evolved. To make sure it was not seen as a trick, Ben would have to enter and make his way to the front of the United Nations auditorium, but not on the usual platform. Ben would have to be on the main floor within touching distance of all the world's leaders. He would make a speech which Lizzie had written and had been approved by both the CIA and MI6, answer a few questions, and then disappear. If all went to plan, things would go back to normal in a few days and the world's leaders would only slightly distrust each other, but not enough to start a war. If it went wrong, the whole world would believe the Americans and British were behind the whole scam and a World War would start.

"No pressure then, Ben," Lizzie had reminded him on at least three occasions in the last few days, as she put the finishing touches to his speech.

Ben could feel the tension in the air as he made his way to the centre of the auditorium. The rumours were rife that this was all a set up to cover up a failed attempt by the Americans to rule the world.

The costume, it had been decided, would be just as Lizzie had described: a boiler suit used in radioactive laboratories which had a hood that covered his whole head. The face visor had been replaced by a mirror-type cover, so Ben's face could not be recognised, and his voice had been altered to sound as inhuman as possible. It was also sprayed with a coating of the anti-scanning paint and a small amount of the purple smoke was also placed on the suit. The suit would be analysed by a large team of scientists from all around the world, so they needed to make it as convincing as possible.

After shaking hands with seven or eight leaders to prove that there was someone in the suit, Ben started to recite his speech which he had learnt like they were lines from a one man play. He was very much alone in front of the entire world.

"Just stay calm," Ben he kept saying to himself, "don't disappear too early."

We are from a distant planet many, many suns from your sun," Ben started. "We have studied you and your communications, so have chosen the language of English to let you know we mean you no harm. This is not what we look like; this suit is being used to protect me from your planet's germs and viruses. My race has been sending crafts to all parts in search of life and resources. After studying your planet and its people, you have nothing we need or want, so we will be leaving you alone. You are very aggressive by nature, and will probably destroy yourselves very soon anyway, either through war or your climate changing. You will have violent storms and your food will run out sooner than you think." Ben thought that was a nice touch by Lizzie to promote climate change through this global audience of 6 billion viewers.

"That is why," he continued, "we will not leave you with any of our technologies or weapons. We will not assist your destruction."

You could feel the tension building as it seemed as though everyone was being taken in and believing what Ben was saying.

There was then supposed to be a question from Russia followed by China and then the USA, but the deafening noise of over 200 delegates shouting at once was too much for Ben to hear clearly or speak and be heard.

Then, without notice, the boiler suit fell to the ground in a heap. The whole auditorium stood in disbelief.

"It's a trick!" someone shouted out. This echoed around the auditorium and was repeated by more and more voices. A small delegation of leaders came down to inspect the empty boiler suit and the floor beneath. Others were watching back the pictures on television monitors of the disappearance in disbelief. Little groups huddled together discussing what they had just heard and seen. If it was a trick, how was it pulled off on the floor of the United Nations, and by whom and why?

After watching the pictures on the monitors over and over again, the world leaders started to disperse. It had worked. There were always going to be noises of conspiracy, but not enough for two countries to go to war. You could never convince everyone. Magicians around the world would be shown the pictures of the alien disappearing to see if it could be done or if it was a trick.

Ben reappeared in the offices of the CIA in New York where Michael Grant and Robert Jenkins-Smyth were waiting.

"Well done, Ben," Michael said. "You did a great job. Most of the delegates are going to report back to their people convinced the aliens have left. There will always be some who will never believe, but once there are no more sightings, they will leave things alone. You must never be linked to what happened here today. In fact, Ben you must not be seen by anyone in New York. After all, you are famous for saving the president's daughters life. You will be recognised; we can't take any chances. Ben, you must become invisible again. We will then take you back to Area 51 where the tests will continue."

"How much longer am I going to be kept at Area 51?" Ben moaned. "I feel like an innocent man being kept prisoner."

"We need to discover what has happened to you, Ben," Michael Grant replied. "You must understand how important this is. The technology will put Britain and America ahead of the world and that will lead to world peace."

More like world domination, Ben thought.

"I will go back to Area 51 and make myself available to the scientists," Ben said. "But for the next three weeks, only until my eighteenth birthday. I want to continue my life, and you can't keep me indefinitely. I saved the world and helped you cover everything up. If you try to keep me forcibly, then I will go back to the United Nations and show them what I can do."

"Don't threaten us, Ben," Michael Grant said. "That would be a very foolish thing to do. A very foolish thing, of that I can promise you."

Ben knew they could keep him drugged so he could not disappear, or worse still hurt his father or Lizzie. He would have to co-operate for now.

THIRTY

"Good news, Ben," Lizzie said, "I have managed to persuade Roberts Jenkins-Smyth to allow me to visit you for your eighteenth birthday next week."

"How did you manage that?" Ben asked. "I don't care" he continued, "it would be great to see you. It's been so long. I really miss you."

"32 days" Lizzie answered immediately. "I miss you too. I think they are worried you might disappear if you are not kept happy, so I'm being used to cheer you up. On this occasion, I don't mind being used. Any news on the tests so far? It's all so top secret now that no information is available unless you have the very highest clearance."

"No," Ben replied, "Even father and Professor Antony, I mean Marie, are scratching their heads in amazement at the technologies these aliens possess. I'm hoping that they will let me return to London soon. I'm trying to convince the CIA and MI6 that I would be available to assist in any mission as long as I have my freedom. They could drug me up and keep me hidden away, but the thought of having an invisible spy is too much for them to ignore. I would become a modern real-life superhero."

The last few days before Ben's birthday had really dragged, but the day had now arrived, and he was looking forward to seeing Lizzie again. Ben didn't feel any different now he was a man, just anxious to leave Area 51. After all the hard work of trying to break into the base, he never once thought that he would be a prisoner there himself. There would be no alcohol at his party, which had been arranged by Professors Norton and Antony, because he was still underage in America. Lizzie arrived with some presents which Ben duly opened; he had a smile the width of his face, not for the gifts, which were lovely, but because Lizzie was there. That's when it dawned on him how much he cared for her.

The party was nice, but Ben was glad it was over. It was late and Lizzie was tired and about to head off to her room for the night. Ben had another idea. He said goodnight to Marie and his father, then made his way back to his room. He put on his special white t-shirt, jeans and trainers and made himself invisible. He floated down the corridor towards Lizzie's room. Ben didn't want to just appear in her room, she might think he was a pervert or something. He reappeared outside her room and gently knocked on her door. Lizzie opened her door and was pleased to see Ben standing there.

"I hope you don't mind," Ben said. "The night is still young" as he entered her room.

"No, I'm glad you are here," Lizzie replied, with an enticing smile.

Ben closed the door behind him and slowly approached Lizzie, trying to be as careful as possible. Now was not the time to trip up. Lizzie was now standing by her bed; she looked more beautiful than ever, her big blue eyes sparkling like giant diamonds. As Ben gently leaned over to give her the kiss he had been dreaming of on her luscious lips, he disappeared.

 Matador

For exclusive discounts on Matador titles,
sign up to our occasional newsletter at
troubador.co.uk/bookshop